Lying Tongues

& Frosted Buns

Book 2 in the Church Lady Mysteries Series

By

VJ Dunn

HEA Publishers
PO Box 591
Douglas, AZ 85608-0591
Or email: author@vjdunn.com

Table of Contents

Chapter 1

There are six things the Lord hates,

seven that are detestable to him:

haughty eyes,

a lying tongue,

hands that shed innocent blood,

a heart that devises wicked schemes,

feet that are quick to rush into evil,

a false witness who pours out lies

and a person who stirs up conflict in the community.

Proverbs 6:16-19

"I'M GOING TO BE A LESBIAN!"

I tripped on my own two feet at that declaration. I couldn't say that was something I ever expected to hear coming from my best friend, and, judging by the strange looks she got from our bakery customers, they never expected to hear that from her either.

"You're what?" I asked a little too loudly while glancing up when I heard the door chime. I grinned when I saw Robert walk in. I had to admit, it was nice to have a boyfriend, though I realized I needed a better title for the man. "Boyfriend" just didn't quite cut it for a man drawing a pension.

"I'm going to be a lesbian!" Maggie repeated as she did a little dance behind the counter. She'd been spreading icing on cookie bars when her phone rang, and I was too busy waiting on our customers to pay attention to her end of the conversation.

"And that's my cue to leave," Robert said, spinning on his heel to head back out the door that hadn't even closed yet.

"Hold up!" I laughingly called. "I might need backup for this one."

Robert seemed a little reluctant when he turned around, his broad shoulders dropping as he walked up to me and kissed my cheek. "Do I want to know?" he murmured in my ear before taking a seat at the counter.

"Darned if I know," I told the guy, then moved around the counter to help Maggie. The place had only been open for a few weeks, but we'd been swamped since day one. Being the only bakery within a twenty-mile radius meant all the locals headed our way whenever they wanted a special treat.

I poured Robert a cup of his favorite coffee, one I made sure we ordered several cases of since it was difficult to come by. And once it brewed, nearly everyone who had a sense of smell wanted a cup. Even people just walking by the bakery would get a whiff of the coffee and would head on in.

I hadn't done our books yet—that was a task I had been dreading—but I was pretty sure a good portion of our profits would be due to the Sumatra coffee.

Once Robert was on his way to being properly caffeinated, I turned toward Maggie and propped a fist on my hip while I leaned against the counter. Thankfully, she had stopped that ridiculous dance of hers and had gone back to icing the bars, though she continued to weave and bob while swiping her spatula over the tops of the cookies.

"What's this about being a lesbian?" I asked.

Maggie was sprinkling blueberries on the icing for her delicious blueberry lemonade bars, and she glanced up with a grin, before noticing Robert had taken a seat at the counter. "Hi there, Chief!"

Without looking at the man, I knew he rolled his eyes. Most of the town still called Robert "Chief", even though he had retired from the Crown Hill Police Department many moons before. Maggie, though, had no excuse, since she'd only moved to our town after Robert had retired.

"Hey Maggie," he muttered as he sipped his coffee. I reached over and snagged one of Maggie's bars, then put it on a plate and set it before Robert. He grinned at me as he took a bite.

"Enjoy it, because that's the only sugar you're getting today," I told him with a pointed look. The doctor warned him that his blood sugar was on the rise and to cut back on carbohydrates, particularly the sweets. It didn't sit well with Robert, because the man definitely had a sweet tooth.

Instead of the frown I expected, he grinned. "I bet I can get some sugar from my woman," he said with a wink. "What do you think of that, Maddie May?"

"My, it's hot in here, isn't it?" I spun around, fanning myself. Robert chuckled behind me.

"So?" I prompted my friend. She glanced up at me again, her dark gray brows furrowed. I knew that look; she had no idea what I was talking about. I sighed.

"You're going to be a lesbian," I reminded her. "Wanna explain how you came to that decision?"

Maggie grinned again, then put her spatula in the sink. I took the tray of treats and slid them into the counter's display case while she washed her hands.

"I went to the community theater the other day," she said over her shoulder. "You remember... I told you I won tickets from the radio station, but you didn't want to go to the play with me, so I asked Dottie."

Stupidly, I felt a twinge of jealousy at the mention of our mutual friend. Dottie and Maggie had gotten extra chummy since Robert and I had started dating and I wasn't as available for Maggie and her stupid ideas as I once had been.

Maggie needs a man so we can double-date. I almost choked on the thought that flitted through my brain just then. I wasn't sure Robert could handle Maggie for that long. While he liked

3

the woman, she tried one's patience. Most days, I barely stopped myself from shoving her head in the big mixer and giving it a whirl. At least then she'd have an excuse for her jumbled thoughts.

Maggie shut the water off and turned back around while drying her hands. "You should have gone with me," she added with a pout. I hated it when she did that; the bottom lip stuck out on her aged face was not attractive, though I was sure Maggie thought she looked cute. "The musical was great!"

I stared at her for a moment. "First of all, King Lear is not a musical. Second—"

"They sang," Maggie interrupted. "So yeah, it was a musical."

"What I mean is, King Lear should never have been made into a musical!" I snapped. "It's ridiculous! I can guarantee Shakespeare never intended his tragedy to be performed to eighties pop music." Seriously, it was the lamest thing I'd ever heard of when I read the play's billing. "That's why I didn't want to go with you."

Maggie shrugged as she put her drying towel on the rack. "Whatever. Dottie and I met Angelina Jolie–"

"You met Angelina Jolie," I drawled... an incredulous statement, not a question.

"Cholie," she corrected. "She's the lead in the play. And she's the reason I want to be a lesbian."

I blinked a few times at that, not really sure how to respond. Strangely, the first thing that came to mind was the fact that a woman was playing King Lear and that she'd taken a stage name that was close enough to the famous actress that she was likely heading for a lawsuit. My mind mostly couldn't wrap around the last part though.

A quick glance at Robert proved he had no idea either, as the coward was pointedly sipping at his coffee while he tried not to laugh.

Maggie's statement—heck, nearly every statement by the

woman—required a deep breath before replying. I took three.

She headed to the flour bin, so I knew she was going to start making her nearly famous Sweetie Pie Rolls. They had nothing to do with pie, but Maggie insisted on the name, stating the rolls were a southern recipe and needed a southern name. Regardless of what she called them, the rolls sold out every single day, no matter how many she made.

I'm not a great baker, so I left most of that to Maggie, but I helped out where I could. I attached the dough blades to the giant mixer we bought second-hand while she measured out enough flour to make rolls for an entire Army battalion.

"So, back to your story," I prompted over my shoulder. I really needed to get to the bottom of the "lesbian" thing, though I wasn't too sure why I wanted to do so. While I might be old-fashioned in my morals and ethics and whatnot, I also felt that I was somewhat progressive. If Maggie wanted to make a boyfriend out of a girlfriend, who was I to say something?

"Hmm?" Maggie asked absently while she retrieved the milk and eggs from our big refrigerator, yet another second-hand item. In fact, the only thing we bought for the bakery that was brand new was the commercial oven, which cost more than my first house had back in the early seventies. Despite that, we managed to open the bakery under budget and a good month before we'd planned, thanks to Todd Evans, our contractor friend.

"Your story?" I prompted as I moved back to the counter and turned around to watch while she cracked eggs into the big glass measuring cup. I'd never done such a thing myself—just cracked them into whatever I was making—but Maggie said it was the only way to make sure you didn't get shells into whatever you were cooking. I had to admit, I'd felt rather dumb that I'd never thought of it in all the sixty-something years I'd been cooking.

"Oh, yeah!" Maggie said with a bright grin. "So, Dottie and I met Angelina after the show, and she told us she was going to produce another play in a few months and said she was starting auditions." She stuck her considerable chest out then as she straightened her spine and turned my way with a self-important look on her flour-dusted face.

"Angelina said that I had what it took to be a star," she said with a sniff. My lips twitched while Robert snorted behind me.

"That so?" I drawled. "And what would that be? A fat checkbook?" My comment made Robert choke on his coffee and I turned to toss a napkin at him with a grin. He wiped his chin with a look that said he was barely keeping it together; any moment, he was likely to be on the floor in a hysterical fit.

A confused frown crossed Maggie's face. "My checkbook isn't fat," she argued. "It's thin enough to fit in my wallet."

I sighed as I stared at her. She shrugged and then picked up the measuring cup. "Where was I? One, two, three..." I waited for her to count the eggs as I pursed my lips and tapped the counter behind me with my finger. Robert once said when the Good Lord was handing out patience, I was in line for seconds on stubbornness.

"Eleven," Maggie finally announced as she reached for another egg.

"And?" I said, more snappishly than I meant to.

"Hmm?" Maggie said again with a glance over her shoulder as she dumped the eggs into a big bowl. She picked the milk jug up and started measuring out what she needed.

"Finish your story!" My back teeth were starting to ache.

Maggie jumped. "Oh, yeah. Angelina is so sweet, and really pretty too. I just love her! So, I'm going to be a lesbian!"

That comment was even louder than the one she'd made after getting off the phone, so those who hadn't heard her the first time certainly did that time. There was a spattering of snickers from the room.

I stared at her. "Let me get this straight... you found this woman so attractive that you want to be a lesbian?" As man crazy as Maggie was, it was really implausible.

Maggie tilted her head at me. "She is pretty, but that doesn't have anything to do with me being in the play. She told me that

6

I could have a part in the play without even auditioning! She's so nice," she said again.

I took a few moments to process. "Ah," I grinned with a glance at Robert who still looked confused, "you're going to be a thespian." My man chuckled behind me.

"That's what I said." Maggie gave me a look that said she thought it was me who was a few fries short of a Happy Meal. It was likely the same look I gave her about three dozen times a day.

The door chime rang, and I glanced over to see a strange man walk in. While Crown Hill was small and I knew practically everyone who lived in our town, we were in the midst of tourist season, which meant our little town exploded to more than twice its normal size. The tourists were good for business, at least.

"How may I help you?" I asked when the man took a seat at the counter a few stools down from Robert.

The man was middle-aged and had a harried, weary look about him that tugged at me. I wasn't as caring and compassionate as Maggie—or as I should be—but even a grouchy old broad like me could sympathize with being plain worn out.

"I need coffee," he said with a tired smile, "and also—"

Whatever he said was drowned out when Maggie turned on the mixer. I rolled my eyes, then grabbed a pad and pen I kept for just that reason, handing it to the man.

"Just write it down!" I yelled. The mixer was impossibly loud, probably because it was made back in the sixties. Robert jokingly said it was steam-engine powered and had likely been used for crushing granite. Though that was ridiculous, the thing was a beast. A very loud beast.

When we were planning the bakery, I'd told Maggie I thought we should put the mixer in the back room just for that reason, but she'd insisted that she wanted to be where the customers were as much as possible. With her penchant for flirting with any and every male who walked into the place, I knew exactly why that was.

Which was another reason I wanted to get to the bottom of the lesbian comment, but it was going to have to wait since I had an order to fill. I looked at the notepad to see the worn-out man had written "longo hack copple and chevy seare." I turned and grabbed a large mug from the shelf, then pulled out a cherry scone from the display case. I set both in front of him just as Maggie turned the mixer off. He grinned as I poured the coffee into his mug.

"Most people can't read my writing," he said as he took a tentative sip of the coffee. His face lit up as he held the cup in front of him. I knew the question before he asked it.

"It's Sumatra," I told him as I nodded toward Robert, noticing he needed a refill himself, so I topped his cup off. "You can thank this man over here for that delicious java. And as for the writing..." I shrugged. "I always said my husband had missed his calling and should have been a doctor. Chicken scratch was more legible."

The man laughed as he took another sip, then lifted his cup toward Robert in a salute. "Well, thank you for training her so well."

Robert and I both laughed, though my face heated again at the implication. "My husband is dead," I told him. Funny, but saying that out loud no longer hurt like it used to. Back before I found out Frank was a two-timing no-good hypocritical pastor, just thinking about his death would cause my chest to ache like I was soon to join him with my own heart attack. But now...

I smiled at Robert. He was a big part of the reason it no longer hurt to think of Frank. But also finding out about Frank's infidelity had helped me get over him as well. A bit like ripping the proverbial bandage off the wound.

"Well, my condolences," the man said, looking a bit contrite. He concentrated on his scone, as if he was too ashamed to look at me.

"It was a long time ago," I told him with a shrug, though he never looked up from his treat. I retrieved the wash rag and wiped the counter where I'd dropped some crumbs.

"So, are you in town with the family?" It was a nosy question, but after Maggie and I had our scare a few months back with a serial killer, I found that I wanted to know as much as I could about everyone I crossed paths with. I ignored the look Robert gave me; he knew what I was up to and had tried discouraging me in my sleuthing more than once. He'd yet to succeed. I saw him shake his head in my peripherals.

Maggie cursed, drawing our attention. Well, it was a curse for Maggie, anyway. "Crud muffin" wasn't exactly drunken sailor material.

"Dagnabbit, will you get out of there, you son of a biscuit!"

Robert sighed and put his cup down, then headed around the end of the counter to help Maggie. The woman could never remember to drop the mixing bowl before she tried to remove the beaters. We constantly had to remind her.

"To answer your question," the man said, drawing my attention back to him. He kept an eye on Maggie and Robert while he spoke. "I'm actually here for a... a writing retreat, I guess you'd call it."

My eyebrows rose at that. "You're an author?" Personally, I loved to read, though Maggie was addicted to the television, most specifically to horror movies. She'd be screeching at whatever monster was on the idiot box while I tried in vain to read.

Some days, I regretted splitting my house in two so she could move in.

The man nodded, then wiped his hand on his napkin before reaching over the counter. I automatically shook it, though that would mean another hand washing. I really hated all the rules and regulations Maggie and I had to follow. Back when we were young, no one cared about germs... and funnily enough, we rarely got sick.

"Allen Rogers," he said, "but I write under James Peterson."

My eyebrows rose; not because I recognized the name, but because it was very similar to one of my favorite authors. Allen must have realized what I was thinking, because a blush ran up his face.

"Yeah, I know. Bad thing is I write thrillers too." He shrugged as he pushed his wire-rimmed glasses back up his nose. "I thought it might be a good way to get, uh, well, readers to find me." He huffed out a laugh. "Didn't really work."

You mean to try and steal some readers, I thought with pursed lips, though I managed to keep my thoughts to myself. James Patterson wasn't going to miss any readers, that was for sure.

Bangs and clattering behind me made me jump and I turned to see Maggie and Robert both bending to retrieve one of the dough blades. Of course, they bumped heads.

I laughed as I turned back to Allen. "Keystone Cops," I muttered, though the man was likely too young to know what I was talking about. Of course, they were way before my time too, but I remembered seeing a short Keystone film before another movie when I was a kid.

"I was thinking Three Stooges," Allen laughed. "Minus one, of course." He looked at me pointedly over the rim of his mug, a grin on his face.

A chuckle escaped me, but the smoke detector in the back room went off before I could respond.

"Oh, my muffins!" Maggie cried as she ran for the back room. Smoke tendrils were already making their way into the bakery common area, so I hurried over to close the door. I walked back to the counter, waving a dish cloth to help dissipate some of the smoke.

Allen stood and hastily took out his wallet, throwing a bill on the counter. "I need to leave," he said, waving me off when I started toward the cash register to make change. "I have asthma," he explained with a nod toward the smoke that was still managing to escape around the door frame.

He'd given me far more money than what his coffee and

scone cost. "Okay, well next time you come in, I owe you a cup and a scone or whatever!" I called out. He responded with a wave as he dashed outside.

The rest of the customers decided to take their items to go, so I was busy fetching containers while worrying about why the industrial fan hadn't kicked on to remove the smoke. At the rate we were going, the Crown Hill Fire Department was going to arrive on scene at any moment.

Once everyone was gone, I knocked on the door. "You two okay in there?" There was a muffled response from Robert that was unintelligible, so I cautiously opened the door. The smoke was thick enough to choke a cow, as Maggie would say, and I coughed and waved my hand in front of my face.

I couldn't see very well, but what I could see nearly stopped my heart. Robert was on the floor, flat on his back while Maggie was sprawled on top of him.

"What in the world are you doing?"

Chapter 2

TO SAY I WAS shocked to see Robert and Maggie in such a compromising position would be a huge understatement. I had a moment of pain and panic, thinking that Robert was no better than Frank and was just another lying, cheating son of a gun, and that Maggie was lower than a skink's belly, but then I realized two things: One, Maggie wasn't moving; and two, Robert looked like he was trying to shove her off, not embrace her.

I rushed over to help him. "What happened?" I coughed from the smoke as I grunted and groaned while trying to tug Maggie off. "Good gracious, I think she's been sampling all her baked goods!" It took several tries, but I finally managed to drag her off enough that Robert could crawl out.

Plopping down on the floor next to Maggie, I squinted through the smoke to watch while Robert stood, then rushed over to a switch on the wall near the door. He flipped it up and the overhead fan kicked on. In just seconds, the smoke started to clear.

"Why was it off?" I wheezed from where I sat next to Maggie. I supposed my first question should have been concern for my friend, but I knew how crazy things happened around her. I was certain the situation was just another in a long line of "You'll never believe this, but..." Maggie stories.

Robert sounded a bit wheezy himself when he answered. "It's by the door. Stupid place for it. I'm sure one of us turned it off, thinking it was a light switch."

I made a mental note to fix that problem right away. "What's wrong with Maggie?"

"She tripped over my foot in the thick smoke and hit her head."

I winced. "Again?" That made three head injuries for the

woman in as many months. She was going to have scrambled brains for real at the rate she was going. I might have teased her for being a dingy broad, but head injuries were nothing to joke about.

"Did you get the muffins out?" I asked as he helped me up. I pulled my phone out and dialed 9-1-1.

Robert shook his head. "That's not what's burning. Maggie checked them right away and they're fine." He planted his hands on his hips as he stared at the oven while I waited for the dispatcher to pick up. I saw that the oven had been turned off, though smoke still billowed from the sides. So much for our pretty new oven.

"Oh, hey Deborah," I said when the dispatcher answered. She'd been working as a dispatcher for the Crown Hill Emergency Services for as long as I could remember. I wondered if the woman was ever going to retire.

"So, what's happened to Maggie this time?" Deborah asked. I chuckled.

"Banged her noggin again. We're at the bakery."

"I'll send the ambulance your way. Chief there?"

I chuckled. Deborah knew everything there was to know about everyone in town. Since Maggie and I had opened the bakery, Robert hung out with us most days. And since he knew about a lot more things like the oven, it was a blessing to have him around.

"Yeah, he's here. It's his fault Maggie hit her head. His big feet tripped her."

That drew a laugh and I thanked Deborah, then put my phone away and moved over to stand next to Robert. We just stood there for a moment, staring at the oven before I glanced over at him.

"So, are we just going to glare it into submission, or what?"

That earned me a smirk. "I'm just curious what in the world caused the smoke. The muffins aren't even so much as browned."

13

I frowned at that. "Hold on… Maggie put them in the oven over half an hour ago. They should be done."

Robert grunted. "Well, guess we're gonna have to contact the manufacturer of the thing and get a replacement. Something's not working right."

I stared at the oven a bit longer. "Actually, I think it might be Maggie who wasn't working right," I muttered as I stepped to the oven and bent over. She only used the upper two ovens because she said it was easier to put the trays into, and I had a sneaky suspicion… I opened the door.

"Yep, just as I thought." I straightened and pointed at the smoldering charcoal mess in the oven. Robert leaned over and peered in.

"What in the world?"

"My bet is on melted packing material," I drawled as he stood and looked at me. "Remember when we got the oven and Maggie was so excited that she couldn't wait to use it?" He nodded. It had arrived two weeks prior, and she'd baked a big batch of cookies right away.

"Well, she's the one who unpacked it after the delivery men took it out of the crate. I'm guessing she only removed the packing material from the upper ovens and somehow turned on one of the lower ones by mistake when she was baking her muffins."

Robert gave me a look. "So, what you're saying is Maggie's muffins are only half-baked?" he asked with twitchy lips.

I rolled my eyes. "Hon, that woman's muffins aren't baked at all."

"I heard that," came the muffin head in question's voice. She moaned as she rolled onto her side and tried to push herself up.

"Just lie still," I ordered. "Ambulance is on the way."

I expected an argument, but she surprised me when she rolled onto her back and blinked up at me. "Oh, I wonder if Doctor Haversham will be on duty today. He is so handsome."

The look I gave Robert made him burst out laughing and he was still shaking his head when he walked back out into the bakery's common area. I heard him talking to someone and wondered how in the world the ambulance could have gotten there so fast, but then I realized it was a customer.

"Stay here," I told Maggie as I moved toward the door. I had a second thought and glanced back at her. "If you really play up the helpless act, I bet Paul and Marc will carry you out of here." I laughed at the contemplative look she got. The town's day shift EMTs were young enough to be her grandsons, but that didn't stop Maggie from flirting outrageously with them.

"Cougars should retire when they start getting Social Security," I quipped as I walked out.

"You're just jealous I look so good in animal prints," Maggie responded, surprising me with the quick response. Usually, jokes went over her head.

I was still laughing when I walked out and saw Robert pouring a cup of coffee for a young girl. I smirked when I saw him hand it to her and she frowned into the blackness in her cup.

Taking the cup back, I winked at the girl. "Lacy wants a latte," I told the man. Of course, that earned me a very confused look. "Mostly cream, very little coffee."

"With vanilla syrup," Lacy added. Robert shook his head and walked down the counter.

"I'll leave you two ladies to the foo-foo coffee. I'm gonna wait out in the fresh air for the ambulance. Too smoky in here."

Of course, that led to questions from the young librarian who had been coming into the bakery at nine a.m. every day since we opened. She was addicted to her lattes, and to Maggie's "Macon Bacon" donuts. I hadn't even tried the things... peaches and bacon in a donut just did not sound good to me, but they were yet another big seller. I pulled one out of the covered dish behind the counter and handed it to her before she even asked.

"Had to save you one," I grinned at her. "Missus O'Bryan

wanted a whole dozen and I swear she ate three before she even made it to the door."

"So... what's the story?" Lacy asked. "It smells like someone lit a burn barrel full of diapers in here." Despite the comment, she took a big bite of her donut.

I winced. "I didn't realize it smelled that bad." I'd have to send Robert to Devore's Hardware to get some heavy-duty air fresheners. "We had... an incident with the oven," I said with a literal tongue-in-cheek look that made Lacy laugh.

Lacy grinned and swallowed her bite. "Maggie?"

I nodded, but it wasn't without my own grin. The whole town knew how my best friend could be a bit ditzy.

Before I could explain what had happened, the door to the back room opened and I frowned when Maggie walked out. "What are you doing? You know the drill... don't move until the EMTs check you out."

She waved me off as she walked to the storage cabinet in the corner. "Well, I certainly don't want them checking me out with my hair in such a mess!" she said as she dug around in her purse. She'd hung a mirror on the back of the door and Lacy and I watched while Maggie took a pick and fussed with her hair. Honestly, it looked no different when she was done. With her tight gray curls, I always secretly thought her hair looked a bit like a Brillo pad.

It occurred to me then that the woman had just basically brushed her hair in the same area we made food. *Gross.* I made yet another mental note to get Robert to help me move that cabinet into the back storeroom, next to the restroom. The last thing we needed was a health code violation thanks to Maggie's vanity.

The sound of a siren could be heard then and Maggie squealed before slamming the cabinet door, then hurried to the back room. Lacy and I watched as she got back down on the floor, yanked her blouse down over her stomach, and let out a pathetic moan.

"You're not in the play yet!" I called out. "Save the acting for the stage."

"Shh!" Maggie hissed at me with a glare, then folded her hands on her chest. She apparently changed her mind— probably remembering that was the traditional pose for corpses—then laid her arms out at the side, adjusting them several times. I rolled my eyes as I looked back at Lacy, who raised an eyebrow.

"Another head injury?" she asked as she sipped her latte. I laughed.

"Woman's gonna be as loopy as the rollercoaster at the State Fair if she cracks her skull one more time." Lacy coughed on a laugh, along with a bite of her donut.

"I heard that," Maggie called out.

MAGGIE WAS MOST put out that the EMTs decided she didn't need to go to the hospital. In fact, Paul said he couldn't tell that she'd even hit her head. Of course, my suspicious nature kicked in.

"Were you faking that injury so you could throw yourself on Robert?" I snapped at her once the men left. We were in what we'd come to realize was the "lull" for the bakery—mid-afternoon, after the breakfast crowd and before the after-school rush. We'd fallen into the routine of scrubbing the place down during that time, though my aching back protested every swipe of the mop.

"Of course not!" Maggie protested, a little too vehemently. I paused in the mopping and turned to look at her where she was cleaning the glass case.

"Maggie," I growled in warning. If that Donna Juan was after my man, we were going to have words. Serious ones.

She stopped rubbing at the glass and looked over her shoulder with wide eyes. "No, I swear," she breathed, clearly afraid of me. As she should have been. I believed her, but then she sucked in the corner of her bottom lip and started chewing. I knew that was a sign she had something to tell me that she really didn't want to voice.

I planted my fists on my hips, letting the mop handle fall.

Maggie dropped her paper towel and held her hands up. "No, I swear. It had nothing to do with Robert. But... I did fake the injury."

"What? Why?" Maggie did some ridiculous things, but I couldn't fathom why she would do something so asinine.

"Well, see, I just..." More lip chewing. "It was just that..."

"Out with it!" I barked and she jumped.

"I wanted a break!" she cried. "I thought a trip to the hospital would get me a few hours of rest." Her eyes filled at that, and for the life of me I couldn't say why, but I rushed over to her and pulled her into my arms.

"This bakery is just so much work," she wailed against my shoulder as I patted her back. "I thought it would be fun because you know how much I like baking, but all the other stuff just sucks! I'm so tired."

I sighed, because she was right. The bakery had been open a few weeks and we'd been going non-stop. Up before dawn to get everything ready for the before-work crowd, doors open at seven, running around like madwomen all day and not closing until six to accommodate the after-work crowd. The only day we were closed was Sunday, but that was the day we went to church.

And that was another thing—even though we had a business to run, one that was occupying most of our time, Maggie and I still had duties at the church. We still cleaned on Saturdays, though it was at night after the bakery closed. And on top of that, we also had our own home that needed cleaning, laundry that needed washing, and pets that were being neglected thanks to our being gone so much.

"And I miss Wally and the cats," Maggie cried, as if she'd

read my mind.

"I know, honey," I soothed. "I do too." I sniffed and nudged her away, though I kept a grip on her shoulders. "We need to pray about this. Ask the Lord to send us some help!"

Maggie nodded as she wiped her cheeks with her fingers. It was childlike, but on Maggie, the gesture was rather endearing. "I'll go first." She reached out and took my hand.

"Lord, we need Your help!" she said, though it was more of a demand. "Oh, sorry, we thank You for making the bakery so successful, but it's too much for us. We have too many hands in the fire, so we need You to send someone here to help us!"

"Yes, Father," I agreed, though I was trying not to laugh at her mixed-up idiom. "This is far more work than we thought it was going to be, especially for two old ladies." I ignored the growl Maggie gave at that; she hated to be reminded of her age. "So, if you could send someone our way to help out, we'd sure appreciate it."

I paused for a moment, thinking. While we came in under budget on the remodel, we still spent quite a bit on equipment. It would be a while before we were operating in the black, as they said. "Uh, and someone cheap," I added.

The door chimed and we looked up.

I couldn't believe what—no *who*—I saw walking in. "Elle!" I cried as I rushed to the door. Shock and disbelief filled me when I pulled my only child into my arms. Elle and her family lived three states away and I couldn't remember the last time I'd seen her, but I was a bit shocked at how thin she was... and how old-looking.

"Hi, Mom," Elle murmured against my shoulder, in the same spot Maggie had just been crying. I wondered if my blouse was damp.

"Hey, Gramma." I looked over Elle's head and shrieked when I saw Jasmin. Elle pulled back with a wince, rubbing her ear.

"Sorry," I told her before I gathered my granddaughter up

for a big hug. "I can't believe how big you are!" I cried as I released the girl, looked her over, then pulled her in again. She laughed against me.

"I'm twenty-one, Gramma," Jasmin said drolly. "You shouldn't tell a grown woman she's big." That made me chuckle as I released her.

"She tells me I'm big all the time," Maggie said from behind me. The girls both smiled at her. They'd only met once years ago, but Elle and Jasmin liked my friend.

I stood watching as Maggie hugged my girls. Though I was thrilled they were in town—and shocked that they hadn't called first—I was also saddened and angry that it had been so long since we'd seen each other. They never came to see me, thanks to Elle's husband, Carl, and his demanding job, and the last time Maggie and I had visited them, Carl had been off-putting and downright rude at times, so much so that I hadn't wanted to do that again.

Carl had always been an overbearing jerk and I'd begged Elle to break it off with him when they'd been dating. But when she'd gotten pregnant with Jasmin while they were in college, I thought I'd taken the higher moral road by insisting they marry, despite my misgivings about the guy.

I'd regretted that for the past twenty-one years. And I think it's part of the reason Elle and I drifted apart.

But she's here now. "What brings you to Crown Hill?" Maggie asked. I was thankful, because I wanted the answer myself, but wasn't sure how to ask it. Walking on eggshells was never in my repertoire.

Strangely, Elle glanced at me before answering Maggie. "Uh, well, we just—"

"Mom left my dad," Jasmin said as she wrapped an arm around her mother's shoulders. I realized then that Elle looked like she was about to burst into tears. "He's a class A jack—"

"Jasmin," Elle interrupted in warning. My granddaughter grinned.

20

"Jackalope," she amended with a shrug. "We decided it was time to head outta Dodge."

I took a closer look at Elle then. As I'd noted when I first saw her, she was much thinner than the last time I'd seen her. She was what they called "painfully thin." We Kaye women always leaned toward pudginess, but Elle had to be at least sixty pounds lighter than the last time I'd seen her.

The drooping shoulders told me she was either exhausted, uncomfortable, or a combination of the two. And the dark circles I'd noted under her eyes looked more like... bruises.

"Did Carl hit you?" I blurted out before I could stop myself.

A shuttered look came over Elle's face and she glanced at Jasmin, whose jaw hardened. My granddaughter gave me a look that told me everything I needed to know. *We'll talk later*, she mouthed.

I knew two things in that moment... one, Carl Henderson was going to pay. And two, I didn't look good in orange.

Chapter 3

"YOUR BOYFRIEND'S BACK," Jasmin quipped. I looked up with a smile, expecting to see Robert, but my smile faded when I saw it was Allen. Again. The man had been in the bakery every single day for a week, and often, twice a day.

Thankfully, though, Jasmin was talking to Maggie with the "boyfriend" comment.

Maggie made an embarrassing squealing noise that was reminiscent of the time I'd visited a pig farm when I was a teen. I grimaced and glanced at Jasmin, who laughed as she refilled another customer's coffee.

Elle and Jasmin had been a true godsend—and Maggie and I had no doubts God truly did send them—since they'd started working at the bakery. Their presence allowed Maggie and I to catch our breath and have a life again. And the best part was that we only paid them a small stipend; since they'd moved in with us, they were getting free room and board.

But the snake in the grass part of it was that Maggie now had time to flirt more with the customers.

"James!" Maggie called as she rushed across the common area to hug the man. No matter how many times Allen and I corrected her, the woman insisted on referring to him by his pen name.

Allen was a good ten years our junior, but he was good-natured and always took Maggie's flirtations in stride. But I was getting a bit nauseated by it, to be honest.

"For crying out loud," I snapped as she embraced the man, "you just saw him this morning!" Maggie released him and turned to stick her bottom lip out at me.

"I'm just being friendly. It's good customer service."

I pointedly looked at the other customers in the shop. Over the past week, we'd quit having a slow time in the afternoon and tables were filled nearly every moment we were open.

"You didn't hug anyone else when they came in," I said as I stared at her over the top of my glasses. Of course, that meant I couldn't see her clearly, but I wanted to make sure she got the full effect of my glare.

"Yeah," Nando called out from the corner table with a fake whine, "where's my hug?" Alice reached across their table and smacked the old man.

"Your mug is right in front of you!" she yelled as she pointed at his coffee. "Are you going blind?"

"No, but I think you're even deafer than you were yesterday," Nando smirked.

"What was that?" Alice yelled.

"Nothing!" Nando yelled back.

I laughed at the couple who were our neighbors. Once Maggie and I started working more part-time and less full-time, Nando and Alice often asked us to bring them to the bakery. We were happy to oblige, since neither one could drive. Alice was too deaf, and Nando was too old. I always thought the two of them should get together and be more than friends, but Nando had delusions of being some sort of playboy and didn't want to "settle down with just one hottie."

Maggie laughed at the old man and obliged by leaving Allen to cross the bakery and give Nando a hug. Allen grinned as he pulled out a stool at the counter. Jasmin held the pot of coffee up with a questioning brow lift.

"You got it, kiddo," he sighed as he sat. I tossed the rag I'd been wiping the counter with into the sink and dried my hands on my apron.

"How's the book going?" I asked the man. He'd shared that he'd come to Crown Hill to "get away from the crowds" so he could finish his latest thriller. I'd had my doubts that he'd picked a very good area, since Crown Hill was most certainly crowded this time of year, but then he'd said that he'd rented a cabin in the woods. At least he was away from the beachgoers and noise. But with his constant runs to the bakery, I doubted he was getting much done.

Allen shook his head and rubbed his face as Jasmin set a steaming mug in front of him. He wasted no time in taking a sip, sighing in appreciation.

"I do love this coffee," he said as he set the mug back down.

I laughed. "You must, since you drive twenty miles twice a day to get some." I thumbed over my shoulder at the display of bagged coffee beans on the wall. "You could just buy some beans and make it at your cabin."

Allen grinned at me. "But then I'd miss out on all the hugs," he said with a wink at Maggie as she walked behind the counter to stand next to me. Only Allen caught the look I gave him for that, and his grin widened. We both knew Maggie was wasting her time with the man, but she was still clueless.

Maggie of course preened at the comment, but then remembered she'd left cookies in the oven and hurried to check on them. Thankfully, the burned packing material hadn't ruined the thing and we were able to clean it out. And Robert had installed a cover on the fan switch so it wouldn't get turned off again.

"To answer your question about the book," Allen said, drawing my attention back to him, "it's not going. Not at all." He shook his head and scrubbed at his face with both hands, pushing his glasses up on his forehead as he did. The man looked worn out when he'd first come into the bakery; now he looked like he was on his last legs.

"Writer's block?" I asked, though I really didn't care. I was still secretly upset by the fact that the man had intended to trick readers into thinking he was James Patterson.

My question drew a nod. "That, and my cat," he laughed. "Bixby wants to cuddle whenever I'm trying to work. She loves to sprawl all over my keyboard too."

"Oh, I didn't know you had a cat!" Maggie exclaimed, making me jump. I hadn't realized she'd come back.

I mentally groaned; Maggie knowing that Allen liked cats was like dumping a gallon of racing fuel on her flirting fire. The woman was probably hearing wedding bells and planning their honeymoon.

"Yeah," Allen laughed. "She's a total diva too. Thinks my purpose in life is to serve her."

Maggie nodded enthusiastically. "They're all like that," she said. "Why, my girls demand constant attention!"

I gave her a look; for one thing, that wasn't true. Her cats were perfectly content to do their own thing, as long as their food dishes were full, and the litterbox wasn't. But also her cats weren't all females, another thing I could never seem to get through Maggie's Brillo head.

The two started talking about the ups and downs of being slaves to felines, but when they moved to hacking up hairballs, I left them to it. I grabbed a bottle of iced tea from the refrigerator, then headed to the little office area we'd fixed up in the storeroom.

I smiled when I saw Elle typing away on the computer. Frank and I scrimped and saved for years to be able to send our only child to a good college, and I was so proud when Elle had earned a degree in accounting. But when she and Carl had married due to the pregnancy, he'd insisted she stay home with the baby. At first, it seemed like he was a caring man, wanting to do the right thing for his family, but it quickly became evident the man just wanted Elle under his thumb. If she didn't work, she was completely dependent on him... and he set himself up as a dictator.

"How are things looking?" I asked as I stepped behind the desk and set the tea next to her. She grabbed it and opened it, taking a drink.

"Thanks, Mom," she said as she put the bottle back down, then rolled her head and straightened her back. I reached out and started rubbing her shoulders, smiling when she moaned. She'd been picking apart our finances over the past several days.

"You always gave the best massages," Elle said. I laughed.

"If that were true, your daddy wouldn't have spent so much time and money at the massage parlor in Floydsville." I hated to think how much that man had spent over the years in that place. He had a crushed vertebra from an old injury that pained him, though he didn't like to let on about it. I'd only found out he was getting regular massages when I saw the credit card bill. Frank always insisted on paying the bills, and I suspect that was one of the reasons. He didn't want me to know he was hurting.

Elle gave me a pained look over her shoulder. I stopped the massage and sat in the chair next to the desk.

"What?" I frowned.

She sighed heavily. "You do know that a massage parlor isn't exactly for massages, right?"

I'm sure the look I gave her was nothing but confusion. Elle sucked in her lips, her trait when she didn't want to tell me something. The last time I'd seen it was when she'd come to tell us she was pregnant.

"Elle," I said in warning.

My daughter's shoulders lifted on another sigh, then drooped. "Mom... I really don't know how to say this, but, uh, if Daddy was going to a massage parlor, it was for... well, see, it was because he was wanting... it's just that—"

"Spit it out!" I demanded.

"Sex!" Elle blurted, then put her fingers over her lips for a moment, before reaching toward me. "I'm so sorry, Mom."

I sighed. "Well, darling, I hate to be the one to break it to you, but that wasn't the only place he was playing around," I said, watching as Elle's eyes widened. "Turns out, your father was a bit of a horny toad."

"Mom!" Elle huffed with a laugh. I shrugged.

"It is what it is. Truthfully, finding out about it helped me finally get over my grief." I grinned. "And now I have Robert."

Elle smiled softly. "He is a pretty great guy. You've changed since you've been dating him. You're... softer. Nicer."

I returned the smile while huffing a laugh. "Robert is a good guy," I said as I reached over and patted her hand. I wasn't sure how to respond to the other comment about being softer and nicer. Truthfully, I wasn't sure I liked the idea. I'd always been known for my brutal honesty and I rather liked that most people were a bit afraid of me.

"And the Lord will bless you with a good man someday too."

Elle laughed, though she had a haunted look to her. "I don't think so," she said with a shake of her head. I didn't argue; she'd just barely left Carl and hadn't even started divorce proceedings. It was another thing I wanted to encourage her to do, even if I had to pay for the lawyer. Getting on with her life was most important.

"Back to the finances," she said, turning back to the computer and pointing at the screen. I leaned over, though I really had no idea what I was looking at. When Frank had been pastor, I'd kept the books the old-fashioned way, on paper.

"Now, your operating expenses are low, which is good. But here—" Elle went on about financial stuff I didn't really understand. I had a rudimentary knowledge of such things, but since I'd only done the books for a non-profit, I was a bit clueless when it came to business matters.

"You're so great at this," I gushed when she was done with the explanation I hadn't really paid much attention to. But I was thrilled when she'd told me that the projection was Maggie and I would be making healthy profits from the bakery. Impulsively, I stood and leaned over to hug my daughter.

"It's been a real blessing having you here."

Elle sniffed and I pulled back, frowning when I saw the tears that had gathered in her eyes. I reached out and tucked a strand of her long hair behind her ear. She'd always had such beautiful hair, but it had lost its luster. Much like Elle herself had seemed to.

"Thanks, Mom," she whispered. "I'm glad you're letting

Jasmin and me stay with you for a while."

I made a dismissive noise and waved my hand. "You two can stay as long as you like! We love having you," I smiled. It was true; Maggie was thrilled to have the girls with us, and Wally was his usual nutty self with the extra hands to give him belly rubs. Even Maggie's cats came out more often when Jasmin was around. Of course, that was likely because she was a bit allergic to cats.

"Plus, we most definitely needed the help with the bakery. It was a bit too much for us." I paused, wondering if I should say what was on my mind without talking to Maggie first, but I knew she'd agree. "If you and Jazz want to make it permanent, we'd be thrilled to have you stay on."

I grinned, but Elle's chin wobbled, and I was afraid she was going to start really crying. Pretending I didn't notice, I made excuses and said I'd leave her to "the books" and headed back out into the common area. I hated tears, especially from my kin.

Maggie was still chatting with Allen, which made me scowl. The man kept complaining about not getting his book written, but he spent an awful lot of time not writing. And whenever he was around, Maggie didn't do anything, and she had more rolls to make for the after work crowd that wanted them for their dinner.

"Shouldn't you be getting to the rolls?" I asked her. It was already two o'clock and the rolls took quite a while to rise, plus baking time. She glanced at me over her shoulder, lips pursed. She then turned back to Allen and murmured something to him that I didn't hear. His eyes darted my way, then he chuckled before standing.

"Well, I'll let you get back to work, Miss Maggie," he said, then looked at me with a nod. "Miss Maddie. I'll see you ladies in the morning." I waved half-heartedly as he walked toward the door.

"Bye, James!" Maggie trilled with a goofy wave.

"If that man didn't spend fifty dollars a week here, I think

I'd ban him from the place," I muttered as I picked up Allen's cup and plate and headed to the sink.

"I think he's a lovely man," Maggie sighed somewhat dreamily. I had my back to her, so she didn't see the significant eyeroll that comment received.

She walked to the mixer and fussed with the dough blades. I wondered if this would be the day she'd finally remember how to take them out when she was done. Probably not. She turned and side-eyed me over her shoulder.

"I'm going to babysit Bixby for a week so James can get his book done."

I rinsed the mug and set it on the drying rack, turning toward her. "Who in the world is Bix—oh, wait… you're going to babysit the man's cat?" How ridiculous.

Maggie nodded enthusiastically. "Yeah, he's bringing her over this evening." She grinned as she pulled the canister of flour out. "I was hoping you'd make your chicken divan, since I asked him to stay for dinner."

I sighed, though I nodded. Maggie was an excellent baker, though I excelled in meals. I supposed we made a good team in that respect. Since she spent most of the day baking—and flirting—I made dinner every night.

"I'll see if Robert wants to come over too."

Maggie snorted. "Of course, he does. He never passes up one of your meals."

Her comment made me grin. Robert definitely enjoyed my cooking. I was certain he'd put on a good ten pounds since we'd started dating. It was nice having a man appreciate my cooking, though. Frank often looked for excuses not to be around at mealtime.

He was probably at the "massage parlor" I thought to myself, shaking my head. If that man hadn't died, I'd probably have killed him myself. I glanced heavenward at that thought.

Sorry Lord. That wasn't nice. I couldn't be sure, especially since Maggie turned on the mixer at that moment, but I thought

I might have heard a heavenly snicker.

DINNER WAS PLEASANT, which surprised me somewhat. And between Robert, Elle, Jasmin, Allen and me, we finally got Maggie to start calling Allen "Allen" and not James, which was quite an accomplishment.

After we'd cleared the table and Jasmin insisted on doing the dishes, we had decaf coffee and Maggie's famous caramel pecan brownies.

"You need to sell these in the bakery," Robert said through a mouthful. I pursed my lips at his rudeness, which earned me a grin in return. I burst out with a laugh; it was difficult to be upset with the man.

"I would," Maggie said with an appreciative smile, "but nearly everyone in our church has the recipe."

"Maggie makes these nearly every time we have a food-related church function," I explained as I held one of the squares up. I'd probably eaten a thousand of her caramel pecan brownies, but I never got tired of them.

"And just about all of our church functions are food-related," Maggie laughed.

"I think I need to join your church," Robert said through another bite.

"Me too," Allen agreed, making us all laugh.

After Allen got his cat settled in with Maggie's "girls"—and thankfully, there was minimal hissing and spitting involved—he told us he'd be by the bakery in the morning.

"Why, I'm shocked," I drawled, making him laugh as Robert held the front door open. Robert had picked the man up so he wouldn't have to try to find my house in an unfamiliar town. My man was considerate like that.

"Yeah," Allen chuckled, "but I'm going to take your advice and get some of those coffee beans. I really need to hole up in the cabin for a solid week and get the danged book done." Three of us turned and stared at Maggie when she made a distressed sound.

"But your hugs—"

"The man has a book to write!" I snapped. "It's just a week, for crying out loud." Maggie's bottom lip pushed out and my finger twitched, wanting to shove it back in between her teeth.

"Hey, that reminds me," Robert said as he turned to Allen, "did you know Edwin Evans is renting the cabin over the hill from yours?"

My eyes and mouth popped wide open. "Edwin Evans? *The* Edwin Evans?"

Robert grinned at me. "Well, if by *the* Edwin Evans, you mean the famous author who writes those thriller books lining your bookshelf, then yeah, him."

"You mean to tell me Edwin Evans is in our town, and you're just now mentioning it?" That might have come out a bit screechy, judging by the wince both Robert and Allen gave me.

"I did know he was in Crown Hill," Allen quickly said. I think he was trying to stop a fight, although I wouldn't have been able to stay angry with Robert. Not for too long anyway. Though I did continue glaring at him, he just grinned back. "I ran into him at the gas station. Old fart wouldn't even acknowledge me when I said hi. He's a self-important jerk, to be honest."

I turned my glare toward Allen. "It's not exactly fair to deduce that just because he ignored you. Maybe he's hard of hearing." I certainly was, and had been accused of nearly the same thing more than once when I just plain hadn't heard someone calling my name.

"No, he heard me," Allen shook his head. "Looked right at me, rolled that cigar around in his mouth, then went back to pumping gas."

"He was pumping gas with a cigar?" Robert asked

incredulously. Leave it to the ex-cop to pick up on the infraction.

"Wasn't lit," Allen shrugged. He paused for a moment and a tiny frown pricked at his brow, like he'd just thought of something. If I hadn't still been glaring at him for disparaging my favorite author, I wouldn't have noticed.

"But he normally smokes like a train," Allen rushed on. "Always has a stogie hanging out of his mouth." Why he thought that was necessary to share was anyone's guess.

Maggie started to ask what a stogie was, but I interrupted her. "Maybe the man just doesn't like being bothered by strangers—"

"I'm not a stranger," Allen cut in. "Evans and I both have the same publisher. Same agent too. We've run into each other a dozen times."

Okay, well that ran the wind out of my argument sails. Still, I didn't like hearing the man talking about Edwin Evans that way. But Robert must have sensed more steam was brewing in my head, because he hurried to usher Allen out.

"I don't like that man," I told Maggie after shutting the door. By unspoken agreement, we turned toward the living room. Tuesday nights were Perry Mason marathons.

"Well, I think he's wonderful."

That comment made me want to trip Maggie, but I refrained. What Elle had said was true, I realized; being with Robert was softening me.

Darn it.

Chapter 4

"I THOUGHT ALLEN would have gotten Bixby by now," Maggie whined next to me. I glanced up, then straightened from where I'd been hunched over, decorating the flag cookies she'd baked for Flag Day. My dots were supposed to be stars, but they looked more like blobs. I said as much.

Maggie glanced over at my work and laughed. "Those are the worst stars I've ever seen," she said. She pointed at the tray in front of her with perfectly shaped stars and straight stripes, unlike my wiggle worms and blobs.

"It's not rocket surgery," she huffed with another laugh and a head shake.

I bit my lip not to correct her as I thought about the situation with Allen. I knew the man was taking advantage of Maggie, but I also knew she didn't mind having another feline around. But it had been more than the week Allen and Maggie had agreed she'd watch his cat. I figured the guy had gotten caught up in the writing of his book and had let time slip by.

"Like one more cat in the house matters," I told her as I stretched my neck. Decorating baked goods was hard work, I had to admit, but it was something I was getting better at. I held up one of the cookies and eyeballed it, laughing when I realized I'd painted only eleven stripes.

"Did you call him?" I asked as I dotted another cookie.

"Of course," Maggie said, sounding put out. "He hasn't answered his phone."

"He's probably ignoring you," I told her.

Maggie harrumphed, not agreeing or disagreeing as she filled the Long Johns with cream. I knew she didn't mind having Bixby in the house; in fact, even I didn't mind the cat. She was sweet, not overly lovable—which I appreciated—and, unlike Samuel Adams, Maggie's rotten cat, Bixby didn't attack my ankles from under the sofa.

Which I really appreciated.

But I knew why Maggie was grumbling, and it had nothing to do with the cat. She wanted to see Allen. It made my back teeth ache.

After finishing my decorating job, I went to the back room to sit at Elle's desk and call Robert. Jasmin worked full-time and was indispensable to the bakery, while Elle came in a few days a week to do the books. She seemed so worn-out that I didn't push her to work harder. The poor woman slept more than she was awake, leaving me to wonder what all she'd gone through.

And every time I thought about it, I pondered all the ways one might murder one's son-in-law and get away with it. I just had to be smarter than the Perry Masons and Jessica Fletchers of the world.

"What's up, cupcake?" Robert's voice chirped, startling me. I'd been so lost in my thoughts, I'd actually forgotten I'd called him.

"Don't call me 'cupcake'," I laughed. "Working in a bakery makes that a bit off-putting."

"Sweetie?"

"Nope," I said with a pop.

"Sugarpie?" he suggested with a voice that told me he was grinning.

"Nope again."

"Honeybuns?"

I burst out laughing. "That would be a definite no." I heard clicking across the line and wondered if he was on the computer.

"Muffin? Dumpling? Sugar Lips?"

"Nothing remotely related to a bakery or baked goods!" I managed to choke out through my laughter.

"Well, that leaves out Snickerdoodle, Cutie Pie and Sugar Mama," he said contemplatively. Despite my laughing, I could hear more clicking.

"Wait, are you googling stupid girlfriend names?" I asked.

"What?" Robert said with fake shock. "I would never. This is all from the heart Honey Batter Biscuit. No wait, that's butter. Honey Butter Biscuit."

"Stop!" I chortled. "Close that window and don't ever go back to it."

"But, Butter Babe, you're my Sweetiepie Face Cake," he whined.

I admit I burst out laughing so loud, I'm sure he had to pull the phone from his ear. "Just for that," I wheezed, "I'm going to make you call me Sweetie Cake Face—"

"It's Sweetiepie Face Cake," Robert corrected, sounding put out. "Get the term of endearment right, for Pete's sake."

"Whatever. I now insist that's what you call me." I tried to sound stern, but it was ruined when I couldn't stop snickering.

We talked for a moment about other things, then I asked him if he would drive out and check on Allen, since he was the only one who knew where the man lived.

"I have a better idea," Robert told me. "Let me take you out to dinner and then we'll head over there and check on him together."

I sighed. "As lovely as that sounds, I promised Maggie I'd make tacos tonight."

"Funny story," Robert drawled, "I was going to take you to El Burro for Mexican. You can get some tacos to go. Or Maggie can come with us. Either way. It's Saturday night, the bakery is closed tomorrow, and you deserve a night out."

If we were forty or fifty years younger, I'd likely be upset about my "boyfriend" suggesting my friend go with us. But Robert and I were more like friends than anything romantic, so it didn't bother me.

"She'd love to get out," I told him. "But she'll probably insist we go to Allen's first so she can invite him to come along too." I huffed out a laugh. "She has delusions of romance and probably thinks we can double date."

"Okay, sounds good," Robert said. It made me smile; I'd known the man for decades and he'd always been so easy-going and pleasant. "See ya later, Sweetiepie Cake Face... err, Face Cake. Dang it, I shouldn't have closed the browser window."

"That's Sweetie Cake Pie Face to you," I quipped. "Wait, I don't want to be a pie face, do I?"

He was still laughing when he hung up.

I WAS RIGHT; Maggie did want to go to Allen's rented cabin first. "Delusions of romance," I murmured, making Robert grin.

"What was that?" Maggie asked from the back seat of Robert's truck.

"Nothing," I waved my hand dismissively as I took in the landscape. We were in the thick woods, with trees so close together you could barely see through them. In a few months, the leaves would turn, and the colors would be breathtaking. Autumn had always been my favorite time of year. Which reminds me...

"We need to start thinking about pumpkin recipes," I said as I half-turned to Maggie. She frowned and Robert laughed.

"It's not even officially summer until next week," he drawled.

I grinned and nodded. "Yeah, I know, but I figured if we get canned pumpkin and pumpkin spice stuff now, we'll get a good deal since it's out of season."

"Oooh, I love pumpkin spice coffee," Maggie trilled. "Maybe I can come up with some pumpkin spice muffins or something."

We chatted about bakery stuff while Robert maneuvered up the winding road that cut through the woods. It was a narrow road with no shoulder whatsoever. It was like whoever created the road took down just enough trees to let two cars pass and not a branch more.

"This would be bad in the winter," I said. Robert nodded.

"That's why they close the road to the thoroughfare come November fifteenth. Only the people who live up here can pass then."

I'd lived in the area for most of my adult life and I never knew that. Of course, I never had occasion to head into the deep woods, preferring to stick to the ocean instead.

"It's a bad road anyway," he continued. "Joggers and bicyclists love it, but they're always getting hit."

I turned more fully toward him. "How do I not know these things?"

He glanced at me. "Because you've always lived in your own little world. After Frank, you just had your church activities and Maggie. And you yourself said you didn't want to read the paper."

"I never said that," I protested, though I was shocked that he'd remembered such a thing. "I said I'd canceled my subscription, but it wasn't because I didn't enjoy reading the paper. It was because that little snot Randy Dixon kept throwing the paper into my begonias and breaking them."

"You can read the paper online now," Maggie said as she tapped something on her phone, then reached over the truck's console to show me. "See? This is the app. I have a subscription so I can read The Chronicle."

I took the phone from her and ran my finger over the screen, seeing current headlines for our town's small newspaper as I did. After a moment, I handed it back.

"You read the newspaper?" I asked incredulously, thinking I really must have been living in my own world, as Robert said. It was a bit disconcerting, especially realizing that Maggie had an interest in current events. I felt guilty for thinking she was a "doughy muffin."

Maggie looked put out. "I might not be the brightest tool in the shed, but I do like to keep up with current events."

My eyebrows lifted further. "Really?" She put her nose in the air and did a little head shake thing that made me instantly suspicious. I knew that look... she wasn't telling me something.

"What exactly do you like to read in the newspaper?"

Maggie chewed her lip as she stared at her phone, but she finally murmured, "I like the comics and the obituaries."

I couldn't help but laugh. "Why the obituaries?" There was no reason to ask about the comics.

"I have to keep on top of the deaths," she said, like I should have known that.

"Okay, I'll play," I muttered, making Robert huff out a laugh. "Why do you need to keep on top of the deaths?"

"Because," Maggie replied, dragging out the word, "I want to know if we have a vampire horde or a werewolf pack show up in town."

I threw my arm over the seat back and turned to stare at her. "How in the Sam Hill are the obituaries going to tell you that?"

She lifted her head, presumably so she could stare down her nose at me. "If there are suddenly a lot of deaths, then you have your first clue there's a monster infestation."

I stared at her for a split second. "Or we could have another serial killer."

Maggie's mouth scrunched up to the side. "Yeah, or that," she admitted as she deflated. But then she obviously thought of another argument as she brightened. "But the obituaries will also tell us how they died—you know, like if there were bite marks on their necks."

Robert laughed, obviously thinking she was joking. I knew better. "They don't usually mention cause of death in obits," I spit out. "And they certainly don't give details!"

Maggie looked like she was about to cry, and I had a

moment of regret for being harsh. "Maybe you need to hang out with Victor and get the scoop first-hand."

"Victor?" Robert asked with a glance my way.

"Rudolf," I clarified. He nodded with a grimace that made me grin. Crown Hill's mortician and acting coroner was a bit strange, too strange even for Maggie.

"What I really need," Maggie said with a haughtiness to her voice that made my grin broaden, "is one of those police radios like Robert has."

I rolled my eyes as I glanced at the man. When Maggie and I had stayed with Robert for a week while the Fishhook Killer was on the loose, she'd been enamored with that police scanner, listening to it constantly. She hadn't even been interested in a monster movie marathon that week.

"I'll see about getting you one," Robert told her, making her wiggle happily in the backseat, while I scowled at him. Robert returned the look with yet another crooked grin.

Silence filled the truck cab as the area darkened the further up we climbed. Even though it was still early evening, it was so dark Robert's headlights came on. I leaned over and looked up, fully expecting to see clouds, but instead saw nothing but trees.

"You would think that the higher up we go, the less trees there'd be," I murmured as I sat back. I didn't like the oppressive feeling of being so surrounded and not even being able to see the sky. It was almost suffocating.

"This patch is mostly evergreens," Robert said, "so it's dark like this year-round. Which explains why most of the pedestrian and bicycle accidents happen around here."

He made a turn into the middle of the trees—or so I thought. But somehow, he'd managed to find what was little more than a goat path amongst all the thick forest growth, just wide enough for his truck's mirrors to clear the trees lining the path. Thankfully, it was just a few moments before we crested a hill, and a small cabin came into view.

"Idyllic, isn't it?" Robert asked as he shut the engine off.

"To say the least," I laughed. Whenever I'd pictured a cabin in the woods, the scene before us was exactly what I'd always had in mind. Quaint log cabin with a covered porch, complete with two rocking chairs, a cleared grassy meadow painted with wildflowers, and an old-fashioned well with a bucket for drawing water.

"I'd hate to have to be the one getting water in the winter," I said as we climbed out of the truck. The well was a good twenty yards away from the house, and I cringed at the thought of trudging through the snow to reach it.

Robert grinned over his shoulder. "That's just for show. Believe it or not, the cabin has indoor plumbing." I started to ask how he knew, but Maggie interrupted me.

"Thank the Lord!" I glanced at her, and she smiled apologetically.

"I have to pee."

The cabin was dark, and no sound could be heard from within. Robert knocked several times, and yelled Allen's name while I glanced around the area. The man's Toyota was parked between some trees about a hundred yards from the cabin, partially hidden. If I hadn't been checking the area out, I would have missed it.

Robert planted his fists on his hips with a frown. "Well, I think we missed him."

I pointed toward the Toyota. "His car's over there."

He shrugged. "Maybe he went out for a walk."

Maggie was dancing from foot to foot, and I turned to her. "Really, really have to pee now," she said through clenched teeth.

"Didn't you go before we left the house?" I asked, like she was a child needing reminding. She nodded.

"Yeah, but I had two cups of that tea Jasmin likes."

I frowned a bit. "You mean the dandelion green tea?"

"Mmhmm. It's delicious with raw honey."

40

I tucked my chin and looked at her over my glasses. "Jasmin has chronic bladder infections. That tea is a diuretic." That earned me a confused look. "It makes you have to pee a lot."

Maggie said, "Oh," while Robert chuckled, then sighed.

"Well, I don't have a justifiable reason to break down the door," he said.

"You're not a cop anymore," I reminded him drolly. He laughed.

"No, but I could also be arrested for breaking and entering without a legitimate concern for the welfare of the inhabitant."

I gave him a look for his legalese, then widened my eyes and blinked a few times as I put my hand up to my ear as I leaned toward the door. "What's that?" I asked comically. "Did you two hear that? It sounded like a cry for help."

Robert gave me a look that said he didn't appreciate my dramatic acting, but Maggie must have thought I was a better actress.

"Oh no!" she said as she reached out and turned the knob, while I muttered I'd been joking.

The door swung open, and she grinned at us. "No breaking and entering necessary." She frowned. "Well, entering is necessary, I guess. I mean, how else are we going to get inside?" With that, she took a step over the threshold.

"James… er, I mean Allen! Are you here? It's Maggie!" she hollered, even though the cabin was tiny, just two rooms from what I could tell. Robert and I followed her inside and stopped in the combination kitchen, dining and living area while Maggie hurried to a door at the end of a short hall.

"Bathroom! Yay!" she squealed. Robert and I gave each other a look before laughing.

"Our little girl is growing up," I said as I pretended to wipe a tear from the corner of my eye with my knuckle. "Going potty all by herself and all."

"A proud moment indeed," Robert drawled.

I looked around the place. There was a sofa and two chairs surrounding a small coffee table that had a laptop on it.

"I suppose the cabin has electricity too?" Robert nodded.

"And how do you know all this?"

He turned toward me with a smile. "Your contractor owns this hill," he said. My eyes widened.

"Todd Evans?"

He nodded again. "Yep. He built a cabin up here to use during deer season, then decided to build three more to rent out to his buddies. But during the off-hunting season, he rents them out to tourists."

"Wow," I said. I had no idea, and sort of wondered how Robert knew all that, but then the man was even more nosy than I was, and he'd taken a liking to Todd when the man had been remodeling my house and then the bakery. I imagine a lot of such things came up in conversation.

"Small world, I suppose."

Robert laughed. "Not really, not in a town our size."

"Yeah, but Todd's from Floydsville," I said. That town was probably four times the size of little Crown Hill.

Robert shook his head. "Nope, he just works out of Floydsville. He actually lives in Cherry Bluff." My eyes widened; Cherry Bluff was basically a subdivision of Crown Hill, right on the beach about three miles from our southern town limit. Exclusive and for the very well-off. I had no idea Todd had so much money; the man certainly didn't put on airs.

I laughed. "You know more about Todd than you do about me."

He stared at me for a second, a small smile tugging at the corners of his mouth. "Darlin', I know everything there is to know about you."

My heart did a little flutter thing that made me wonder if I should get in to see the cardiologist. Feeling my face heat, I made a point of looking around the cabin some more. "Well, that figures, since you're a nosy ex-cop."

That made him laugh. "Look who's talking about being nosy... the woman who interrogates every single customer at the bakery."

I shrugged. "You never know who might be our next serial killer. Heaven forbid," I quickly added.

Robert laughed again, then sighed as he glanced down the hall toward the bathroom. "How long does it take her to use the facilities?"

"Well, depending on what all she's doing in there, anywhere from three to twenty minutes." At the look he got, I hurried to add, "I mean, if she's on her phone playing a game or something."

"Maggie!" I hollered. "Hurry up! I want tacos."

A moment later, we heard the toilet flush and in another moment, Maggie came out, tucking her phone into her back pocket. I shot Robert a look that made him laugh.

She started toward us, then paused at the open door I assumed was the bedroom. Maggie frowned, leaned forward slightly, then put her hand over her mouth and stepped back, hitting the wall behind her. She then pointed with her free hand at something in the room.

Robert hurried toward her with me hot on his heels. When he reached the door and peered in, he straightened, and I bumped into his back.

"What?" I asked. "What is it?" I tried to look around him, but he put an arm out to block me, then reached out and grabbed Maggie by the hand and tugged her toward us.

"What's in there?" I demanded to know, although I had a pretty good guess. It wasn't a "what," it was a "who." And, judging by my friends' reactions, it wasn't a good sight.

Robert pulled his phone out, presumably to call the authorities, while I stared at Maggie. I was half-tempted to force my way around Robert to see things for myself, but I figured if he didn't think I needed to see what was in there, I probably didn't.

"He... there's... it's..." Maggie stammered. I had a moment of pity at the lost, horrified look on her face and pulled her in for a hug.

"What is it?" I couldn't help but ask. I felt a bit guilty, since she was obviously traumatized, but with Robert blocking the narrow doorway, I couldn't see what they had seen. And yes, I had to admit I was nosy. "What did you see?"

"I... I saw..." She pulled back and looked at me, eyes wide and pupils so large, her blue eyes looked black.

"I think there's a dragon in Crown Hill."

Chapter 5

A DRAGON," I deadpanned. Then I realized Maggie was likely in shock and softened my tone. "Why would you think that?"

"Because… b-because… there's…" She sputtered and pointed toward the room. Robert finished his call and looked back at me with a wince.

"Because there's a burned body on the window seat in there," he explained, jerking his thumb over his shoulder.

"Oh," I breathed. Part of me wanted to see, but the smarter, saner part was glad the man had kept me from looking in the bedroom. And despite the fact that Maggie loved all things horror, I was sorry she'd seen it as well.

Robert's mouth was pinched as he led us back outside to wait for the authorities. I knew it was a crime scene and that we shouldn't contaminate it, but I was itching to look around.

We walked back to Robert's truck, and he opened the passenger doors for us. Maggie climbed into the backseat and sat with her arms wrapped around her midsection, as if giving herself a hug. I knew I should probably comfort her some more, but I just felt so antsy. Instead of getting into the truck, I started pacing while Robert leaned against the truck bed, arms crossed over his chest, watching me.

"How could the body be burned, but not the cabin?" I asked as I glanced back at the structure made entirely of wood. The interior, as well, consisted of wood flooring and walls. While it was rustic and homey, it was a death trap in a fire.

Or it should have been.

"Don't know," Robert said as he nibbled on his bottom lip. "You're right, though; that place should have gone up and half the woods with it."

That made me shiver; two years back, we'd had a fire come up over the ridge of the Purple Mountain that threatened our town. We'd all been packed and ready to go in case of evacuation. Maggie had even gone out and bought cat carriers for her herd, just in case. Thankfully, the wonderful wildland firefighters had managed to get it under control.

"Do you think the body was brought here after?" I asked as I stopped in front of him.

He thought about it for the briefest of moments, then shook his head. "No, there were scorch marks on the floor and walls."

I frowned. That was even more strange, that there were burn marks on the wood, yet the cabin didn't catch fire. I glanced at the truck's backseat, then leaned closer to Robert.

"Not to sound like Mad Maggie, but is it possible this was one of those spontaneous combustion things, do you? You know, where a person just turns to ash, but nothing around them burns?"

Robert's look said it all. "I'm not sure that's a real thing," he said. "Never heard of it in all my years on the force, other than on television shows."

I didn't mention that the "force" he was on served and protected a whopping population of only two thousand. More during tourist season, but still... not much of a possibility of running into something so rare. If it was even a "thing."

"Well, what—" My question was interrupted by the sound of a vehicle. I lifted my eyebrows and looked at Robert.

"How did they get here so fast?"

He was staring at the tiny road leading to the cabin and we both watched as a familiar truck crested the top of the hill.

"You called Todd?"

Robert nodded. "Figured since this was his place, he'd want to know what happened."

I frowned slightly. "How'd he get here so fast?" I repeated.

"He was at his hunting cabin just over the ridge."

I saved further questions as we watched Todd get out of his truck. He started around the front, then paused to stare at the cabin for a moment, as if he really wanted to go inside and see things for himself. After a few seconds, he seemed to sigh then headed toward us.

"Do I want to know?" he asked Robert with a wary grin. He glanced at me. "Hey, Maddie."

"Hello, Todd." I liked the young man; he'd treated me very well and fairly during the two projects we'd worked on. Maggie, of course, was enamored with him, so it was surprising she wasn't leaping out of the truck.

Todd's question made it obvious that Robert hadn't told him what we'd found. I glanced at Robert, wondering what he was going to say.

"We have a body here," he finally said.

Todd's eyebrows rose. "Body? You mean… dead?"

Robert nodded. "We're assuming it's Allen Rogers, but we need to wait until the coroner can run some tests."

"Tests?" Todd asked, looking to me for either confirmation or explanation. I didn't offer either one, mostly since I didn't know a whole lot myself.

"I can't say much," Robert grumbled. "CHPD will be here soon."

I fought not to roll my eyes at that; hopefully, they'd send someone more reliable and smarter than Robert's grandson, Jonny Donovan. How that kid made detective for our police department was anyone's guess.

We talked about the bakery for a few minutes, then Todd went to the back door to say "hi" to Maggie. He returned to us in just a moment, a confused look on his handsome young face.

"What's wrong with her?" he asked as he nodded toward the open door.

"Nothing," Robert said while I mumbled, "We don't have enough time to list it all."

It was five minutes later before we heard sirens in the distance. "Hope they find the place," I said as I turned to Todd. "How in the world did you get work trucks up here to build the cabin? That road is hardly more than a bike path."

He grinned at me. "It was twice that size when we built up here. The forest is just taking over again."

We watched as the first vehicle topped the hill, an ambulance. Right behind that was a police car with flashing lights. I was relieved since I thought it was going to be Jonny on the scene, but Jonny drove an unmarked car.

I sighed when I saw Jonny's car right behind the police car.

"Great," I muttered.

Robert looked at me in question. "What?"

"Nothing." It did no good to complain about his kin. Besides, it wasn't nice.

Jonny made sure he was the first one to get out of his vehicle and we headed toward him, meeting him at the side of his car. "Grandpap," he said with a head nod Robert's way as he shoved his suit jacket back to put his hands on his hips. I got the distinct impression he was trying to look important. A preening peacock, if you asked me.

It also didn't skip my notice that he completely and rudely ignored my presence.

Jonny looked over his shoulder at the cabin. "Whatcha got?"

"Body, on the window seat in the bedroom," Robert said. "Burned beyond recognition."

Todd sucked in a breath, and I felt a stab of sympathy for the guy; it was bad enough to find out someone had died inside your property, but even worse to find out fire had been involved.

"Crispy critter, eh?" Jonny said with a chuckle. The grin made his long face look even more comical, though I wanted to slap him for his insolence and insensitivity.

I didn't need to, though. Robert was in his grandson's face in a flash, finger pointing at his nose. "Boy, how many times do we have to go over this? You will be respectful, or so help me, I'll beat it into you!"

Jonny looked back at the other emergency response people with an embarrassed expression. I noticed the others pretended not to notice him getting a dress-down. At least the kid had the good sense to look chastised.

"Sorry," he muttered, then cleared his throat. "Any idea who it is?"

Robert still looked a bit ticked, but he stepped back. "I'm assuming it's Allen Rogers." He nodded toward Todd. "He was renting Evans' cabin here."

Jonny looked at Todd, then nodded. "Good to see you again," he said. Todd murmured something back, though I couldn't hear what it was.

"Why are you here, Grandpap?" Jonny said as he glanced my way. I saw his upper lip twitch, like he wanted to sneer at me but didn't dare with his grandfather present. I stared back at him with a bored expression, which did more to irk him than if I'd sneered myself. He frowned, then turned his eyes back toward Robert, who surprisingly wrapped his arm around my shoulders. Jonny's sour expression made it clear that he did not like that at all.

"I was going to take the girls out to dinner," he said. I chuckled at the "girls" comment, and he gave me a little squeeze. "Maggie wanted to stop by and invite Allen to come with us—"

"And to check on the man," I interrupted. "He hasn't answered his phone for days."

Jonny frowned and actually gave me his full attention. "Why were you in contact with the victim?" he asked with a glance toward Robert. I could practically hear his implication... *She's cheating on you.*

I stared at the boy, which made him twitch. "Maggie was. Not me. She'd volunteered to watch Allen's cat, which was supposed to last for a week. It's been over a week now, and he hasn't come to get the cat, hasn't answered his phone."

Jonny made some sort of noise that I couldn't interpret, then turned toward the cabin. I noticed the EMTs had the gurney unloaded and were struggling to push it up the grassy incline toward the cabin. Robert kissed my cheek.

"Wait here," he said as he left to follow his grandson.

Todd and I both moved back toward the truck and leaned against it, though I really would have liked to sit inside, but I didn't want to upset Maggie further by talking about the death. I also thought it would appear strange if I suggested Todd and I sit in his truck.

"So... how bad is the damage in there?" Todd asked, though I could tell he really didn't want to know.

I shrugged. "I don't know. Robert wouldn't let me see it. But he said the floor and wall were scorched."

"Great," Todd muttered. He straightened, a stricken look on his face as he put his hands up. "I didn't mean to sound so cold," he rushed on. "I mean, it's horrible that Allen died and all—"

I waved my hand dismissively. "No need to explain to me. I feel the same way. Didn't really know the guy, didn't really care for him either, but I'm sorry he's passed. I wonder if he left any family."

A sniffle from inside the truck made me wince and I assumed Maggie could hear us. I looked toward the cabin and tilted my head that way.

"C'mon, let's go sit in those rocking chairs. They look pretty comfy."

"They are," Todd grinned. "I bought them at Cracker Barrel and tried them out first."

Once we were settled—and I made sure I took the chair closest to the door so I could listen in on what Jonny and Robert were discussing—I looked back at Todd.

"It's a good thing your cabin didn't burn down," I told him. "I mean, any kind of fire in a wood structure like this is pretty scary."

He smiled, though he looked uncomfortable and I wondered if it was because we were so close to the dead body. Some people were just like that... didn't handle death well.

"It's not surprising it didn't burn," he said as he rubbed the dark stubble along his jaw. It was obvious he hadn't shaved in several days. "It's mostly made from laminate wood," he explained. "Laminate is inflammable."

My eyes widened. "Well, that's good to know." I had chosen laminate flooring in my home when Todd had remodeled it and was even more glad I did.

He nodded as he reached back and patted the log wall behind us. "Yeah, everything except the outside wall is inflammable, and even this is treated wood, so it won't burn as easily."

I heard Robert and Jonny speaking then and strained to listen to what they were saying, cursing myself for not getting to the doctor to get hearing aids when I only caught a few words here and there.

"How long was..."

"... ask Evans ..."

"... suspects?"

"He was... in town. Don't think he..."

I huffed in frustration and Todd chuckled. I glanced his way, my lips twitching when I realized he knew what I was doing.

He leaned closer. "Don't tell anyone I said this, but I think you'd be a better detective than Donovan there," he said with a head tilt toward the cabin. The comment made me smile, though I shook my head. I had to stay humble, after all. I gave up trying to be covert since Todd was onto me and leaned closer to the door. It didn't really help.

"His car's..."

"...relatives and the like."

"...author, working on a book."

I gave up trying to hear anything inside and decided to try to finagle info out of Robert when we were alone. The last comment gave me pause though.

"Do you have another author renting one of your cabins?"

Todd nodded. "Yeah," he grinned. "A famous one though—
"

"Edwin Evans," we both said together, with a laugh.

"No relation though," Todd shrugged.

I wanted to hear more about the famous author. "What's he like?" Allen didn't seem to like the man much, but I didn't put much stock in the man's opinion. God rest his soul.

He laughed. "He's kind of grumpy, to be honest. I think he just wants to be left alone."

I frowned at that, thinking Todd's assessment lined up with what Allen had said. "Where's his cabin?"

Todd stared at me for a few seconds. I rolled my eyes. "C'mon, I'm not going to stalk the guy! I doubt I could find the place anyway, if it's anything like this," I added as I waved my hand toward the goat path road.

That earned me a chuckle and a head jerk toward the north. "It's over the ridge. My personal cabin is in between this one and the one Edwin's renting."

I nodded, but before I could ask another question about the author, Todd added, "I guess Rogers and Edwin were pretty close friends."

That comment made me want to laugh, but I managed to keep a straight face. "Why do you say that?"

He shrugged his broad shoulders, then leaned back and tucked his hands behind his head. "Saw Rogers driving by my place several times this past week. I had to assume he was on his way to see Edwin, since there's not much else down the road. In fact, it dead ends at the national forest 'bout a mile up."

I bit my lip to keep from admitting that was strange, since Allen said Edwin Evans had treated him with contempt. I mentally shrugged; maybe the two of them had made up.

Todd and I made small talk while we waited, though I kept glancing toward the truck, worrying over Maggie. I was just about to get up and go check on her when Robert walked out, surprising me.

"You're done already?" I asked as I glanced at Jonny behind him. The detective shrugged.

"Not much evidence in there," Robert said. "It's going to be difficult to tell exactly what happened."

Todd stood. "What about the cabin?" he asked, though it was with a wince. "I don't mean to sound cold-hearted," he added with a glance toward me, "but I have another renter wanting the place in a month. Just need to know if I should cancel on them."

"The walls and floor need some work," Robert said. "But it'll have to wait until we get a—" He stopped himself with a wince and glanced at his grandson.

"Sorry," he told Jonny with a self-deprecating grin. "Old habits and all." He put his hand on the young man's shoulder. "Detective Donovan will let you know when the cabin is cleared, and you can get to work on it."

I could tell it pained Robert to walk away and leave Jonny to his job. I had my own reservations about it, especially when I heard Jonny tell Todd it was obviously an accident. He shared that the man had likely fallen asleep with a cigarette since they'd found a lighter on the floor near the body, and that he could start working on the place the next day. I wondered if Jonny had even heard of forensic investigation.

"Not my problem," I murmured to myself as we got into the truck. Maggie still looked a bit shell-shocked.

Robert glanced my way, then at Maggie as he started the truck. "Uh, maybe we ought to just head back to your house," he suggested, widening his eyes at me with a slight head nod toward the back seat.

It was a good suggestion, considering the circumstances. I nodded, but Maggie chimed in. "No, I think I'd like to have a nice dinner," she said barely above a whisper. "Yeah, that sounds like a good idea. Some enchiladas, maybe some guacamole and chips... and a big, tall margarita."

I pursed my lips, because I didn't agree with the consumption of alcohol, but I also knew that Maggie could probably use a stiff drink after what she saw. And, seeing the haunted look in her eyes, I was very thankful Robert had kept me from witnessing it.

Robert nodded, then started the truck and drove back down the mountain. We were all silent, lost in our thoughts, during the ride. I don't know what the others were thinking about, but I know what was rolling around in my own head.

Jonny surmised Allen had fallen asleep while smoking since there had been a lighter near the body. But I was certain Allen didn't smoke, not with the way he'd run from the bakery when we had the incident with the oven. He'd even admitted he had asthma. So, if he didn't smoke, yet there was a lighter in the room...

Was it possible he'd been murdered? But who would want to kill a little-known author holed up in a cabin in the woods? Who even knew he was here? Allen himself had said he'd come to Crown Hill to get away from everyone so he could focus on his writing. He'd made it sound like no one would be looking for him.

But there was the strangeness of Todd seeing Allen driving to Edwin's cabin, assuming that was where he'd been going. Allen had run into Edwin at the gas station, so Edwin knew he was in the area. Allen also alluded to the fact that Edwin didn't like him.

Was it possible Edwin killed him?

I shook that thought off, refusing to think that the author would have had anything to do with it. He was successful, internationally famous. Why in the world would he take the chance of getting caught for the murder of someone so seemingly inconsequential in his life?

But Edwin's so good at writing about murder... maybe it's because he has first-hand experience.

Chapter 6

MAGGIE WAS IN no shape for church the next day, especially since we had to show up early for cleaning before service. After the trauma of the night before—plus the three large margaritas she'd had—I let the woman sleep in.

Wally stood at the door, wagging his tail at me. I looked back at him with a pang of guilt. Even after Elle and Jasmin had started working at the bakery, Maggie and I were still gone far too much. I knew the pets missed us.

I squatted down to Wally's level, ignoring my protesting knees as I wrapped my arms around his neck.

"Be a good boy and watch over Maggie, sweetie." That earned me a tongue to the ear. I grimaced as I wiped it with my shoulder, then ruffled Wally's fuzzy head.

"Mama will come home from church and take you for a nice long walk, okay? And then I'll take you to the ice cream parlor to get a cone." I could swear the dog knew exactly what I was saying, because he started into one of his tornado spins, a sure indication he was happy. I laughed, then hurried out the door before more guilt assailed me.

The church wasn't too bad, thankfully, since all I could give it was a cursory cleaning. I emptied the trash bins in the restrooms, cleaned the mirrors, spritzed disinfectant on the toilets, then headed to the children's building, though I dreaded cleaning it. Maggie usually took that job, which I was always grateful for.

Kids were very messy creatures indeed.

Apparently, all the teachers had thrown parties the week before, because each room needed far more cleaning than I had time for. I picked up a little here and there, but there was just too much mess for one person. After the second room—with three more to go—I got fed up and found a dry erase marker.

I had to admit I was a bit gleeful when I wrote a note on

each teacher's door.

Cleanliness is next to godliness —Book of Maddie Chapter 1 Verse 2, I wrote on the preschool door. And *To clean or not to clean, that is the question. The answer is: Do it yourself!* I wrote on the next door. *This is a self-cleaning classroom... clean it yourSELF!* went on the teens' door. And my favorite: *I just love cleaning messes I didn't make said NO ONE EVER!* I wrote on the middle schoolers'.

I took passive-aggressiveness to a whole new level.

After that, I headed to the sanctuary, ready to tackle that project, though I was dreading it. The pastor was very particular about what he called "God's domain," and had a fit over the tiniest speck of lint or, Heaven forbid, a crooked hymnal in the shelf on the back of the pew.

But once I walked into the quiet, peaceful space decorated in deep blues and dark wood, I had a feeling come over me that I couldn't quite describe. I stopped and closed my eyes, trying in vain to chase the emotion. It took a moment, and then I realized what it was.

Apathy.

It wasn't a happy thought, and certainly could be considered a bad feeling to have, but I knew that—for me—it was good. It was a step in the right direction. And one I should have made a long time ago.

I was sitting on the front-row pew where I always sat, scrolling through a site with funny pet videos Maggie had shown me on my phone, when Pastor Winchester walked in through the back door that led to his office. He grinned at me.

"Good morning, Miss Maddie," he said cheerily. "What brings you to church so early?"

I returned the smile. "Well, I came to clean since Maggie and I couldn't get here yesterday."

The pastor's smile widened as he nodded. "Oh, that's good. Real good..." his voice trailed off when he looked around and the smile quickly fled, being replaced with a sour frown.

"If you cleaned it, why are there still bulletins on the pews from last week?" he asked. He pointed at a spot on the carpet. "And it's obvious the carpet hasn't been vacuumed!"

I paused and glanced where he was pointing. I couldn't see so much as a dust mite, though whatever Winchester saw was enough to make his voice get high and shriekish.

Shrugging, I didn't comment as I went back to my scrolling, grinning when I came across a "Golden Retriever pool party."

"Oh, Wally would love that," I murmured and made a mental note to do something like that for my boy when his birthday rolled around in December.

"Maddie!" the pastor said in a demanding tone. I sighed, paused the video and looked up at him.

"What?" That probably came out far angrier than I meant it too, but que sera sera, as they say.

Pastor Winchester looked a bit taken aback. His mouth flopped open and closed a few times. I supposed it was understandable, since I'd never been anything but respectful to the man. Well, mostly.

I sighed resignedly. "Sorry." I wasn't sure I was being truly sincere, but I really didn't care. That apathy thing had settled in deep.

"Well," the pastor sputtered, "what do you have to say about this?" He threw his hand out toward the invisible aberration on the carpet.

I pushed myself to a stand, put my phone on the pew seat, then crossed my arms over my chest. Winchester took a step back, a wary look in his eye. As well he should.

"What I have to say about 'this'," I said, crooking my index fingers in the air, "is that I've been going to this church since it opened. And why is that? Because I was here when it was being built! My husband and I were the ones who started this church. For the last forty years, I've been here every Sunday, every Wednesday night and nearly every single time those doors were opened," I said as I pointed to the front doors behind me.

"And since my husband's death, I've still been here, still been working for the church, toiling and sacrificing, spending nearly all my free time slaving away. And for what?" I pointed at him.

"So you can complain about an invisible piece of lint? I'm bone tired from running the bakery six days a week and had to get up at the ridiculous hour of five a.m. just so that I could get to the church to clean, only to find out that it wasn't enough. Wasn't good enough."

I took another step toward Pastor Winchester, who backed up again. Smart man. "As of this moment, I'm done. I'm not cleaning any longer, not going to run the missions ministry, or the benevolence, or the decorating committee, or be the acting church clerk. I. Am. Done!"

With that, I spun on my heel and marched to the front doors of the sanctuary. To my dismay, they were still locked, so, head held high, I turned and stomped past the still gaping pastor and headed out the back door.

Once I was in my car, I started laughing. Then crying. Laughing some more. I knew I was hysterical but couldn't find it in me to care. At the moment, I was just... relieved.

I leaned back against the headrest and closed my eyes. "Lord, I'm sorry for the way I acted, and I know You're gonna make me apologize to that man, but right now, would You please just let me wallow? I just want to enjoy my tantrum for a little while."

In all my years, I don't think I'd ever acted that way in front of another person. Of course, in my mind, I'd had all kinds of confrontations. Hundreds of imaginary conversations. But I always leaned toward passive aggression, thinking it was the "high road." Considering the way I was still shaking, it might have been a better idea.

It felt good, though, to get all that off my chest. I'd never stopped working for the church even after Frank died and I was no longer the pastor's wife, the secondary pillar of the church everyone looked to when they wanted something done. Being the "church lady" was most certainly a thankless position, but it was one I had always reveled in. Until now.

I already felt a bit lost.

A knock on the window startled me and I snapped my eyes open, to see Betty Winchester, the pastor's wife, bending over and peering in my window with a concerned look. I sighed and rolled the window down.

"Are you okay, Maddie?" she asked with a soft voice, like one would use when trying not to startle a wild animal. It made me wonder what exactly I looked like at that moment. Half-crazed, likely.

I forced a smile. I had no beef with the woman, though in my opinion she was a bit lazy when it came to church business.

"I'll be alright, Betty. Just... life's just been a bit much lately."

That earned me a kind smile. "I understand."

No, no you don't. The woman didn't hold a job, their kids were all grown, and other than occasionally working with Terrence in the kitchen when we had fellowship meals, she really didn't do anything for the church.

"I—" Betty hesitated, blinking a few times. "I just wanted to say that I'd hate to see you leave the church." To my dismay, her eyes started to fill.

I held my tongue, because I really wanted to say she didn't want me to leave because I did so much, and no one else would be as stupid and gullible as me.

Instead, I smiled. "I'm not leaving the church," I told her. "Well, I am today, because I'm in no condition to sit through service right now." I sighed heavily. "But I have no intentions of leaving permanently. I'm just... a bit burned out."

Betty's head bobbed in agreement, her graying red hair swaying. "I've always said you did too much," she said kindly. "And I always wanted to help you out, but..." She shrugged.

"But what?"

She sucked in a deep breath, as if what she wanted to say

was difficult. "Well, you were just so capable. Large and in charge," she laughed. Her eyes widened then as a horrified look came over her. She put her hand out.

"I didn't mean you're large, Maddie. That's not what—"

I laughed and held up my hand. "I am large, but I knew what you meant."

Betty looked relieved. "Anyway, after Reed and I came here to take over after Frank..." She paused, obviously not wanting to finish the sentence. "Well, you were just so... so competent. You had it all together."

I laughed even harder at that as I shook my head. "I definitely did not have it together, not after Frank died." Honestly, I doubted there was a time when I ever "had it together." Most of the time, I was barely coherent.

Betty smiled. "Regardless, the last thing I wanted to do was come in and take over, you know?"

I looked at the woman in a new light. I'd always thought she was lazy, but now I realized that I might have misjudged her. Maybe she just didn't want to step on my toes. It was enlightening to think Betty might have looked at me like I was competition, being that I'd been a pastor's wife too. And she was kind enough not to try to come in and run me off.

"Doing all the things I did was probably what kept me from falling apart," I admitted. "But now... well, I'm moving on with my life, finally, and I guess it's time for me to let go of the reins." I smiled at her.

"It's your cattle drive now, dear. Good luck getting the herd rounded up."

Betty laughed, then reached through the window to grab my hand. "I'm going to need you to help me," she said with a smile. "Just advice... unless you still want to do the work yourself."

I shook my head. "Maybe just the food pantry and clothes closet," I told her. That was a ministry I'd always enjoyed. "But I'm done cleaning." I nodded toward the church.

"Frankly, your finicky husband is a bit of a pain to please."

Betty laughed even louder as she released my hand. "Don't tell anyone, but Reed is secretly a slob," she said with a crooked grin. "He leaves his dirty underwear and socks all over the bedroom."

That made me laugh. "Well, he sure is picky about the sanctuary."

"That's because it's the Lord's house," she said with a nod. "He feels like we should always give God our best."

Ouch. For the past five years, cleaning the sanctuary had been such a dreaded chore because of the man's obsession with cleanliness. But now that Betty had said that, I felt pretty guilty for my anger about it.

We said our goodbyes and I headed home with a much lighter heart. I was surprised to see Maggie on the sofa, holding a mug of coffee in her hands as she watched a televised service from one of the mega churches. She looked a bit like warmed over dog poo, but I didn't comment. I wondered if the dark circles under her eyes were from crying over Allen's death, or from the effects of three margaritas.

"What are you doing home so early?" she asked, her voice a bit of a croak. I stopped to pet Wally, who spun in circles in front of me. The dog always acted like I'd been gone for days, even if I just walked out to the mailbox and back.

"I kind of had a bit of a meltdown," I admitted as I plopped down next to Maggie. "Told Pastor I was done."

Maggie turned toward me. "What does that mean?"

I stared at the preacher on the television screen, wondering how many times one person could blink in a minute. It made me wonder if he was giving his sermon via Morse Code.

"Other than the food pantry and clothes closet, I'm no longer on any committees." I turned to look at her, smiling. "So we don't have to clean the church any longer."

Unexpectedly, Maggie frowned. "But I like cleaning the church... especially the little kids' rooms."

I laughed, thinking she was joking. I mean, she had to be kidding. That building was a nightmare to clean. But she looked disappointed.

"You can still clean," I assured her. "I'm the one who quit, but I'm sure Betty would love to have you stay on the cleaning team." The "team," which had formerly consisted of just Maggie and me.

Maggie brightened, then looked back at Pastor Blinky. "Good. I love coloring in those picture pages when I'm done cleaning."

I stared at her for a moment. Melinda, one of the Sunday school teachers, had been complaining about someone getting into her room and coloring the master copies for the kids' Sunday school work. She'd thought it had been one of the kindergarteners, judging by the "quality of the coloring."

We watched until the end of the service. My eyelids were heavy from occupying myself by trying to blink every time the preacher had. He must have had eye muscles that could lift a truck.

My stomach growled, probably from all the calories I'd burned while blinking. "You up for some breakfast?" I asked. I knew the one and only time I'd been hungover—thanks to Maggie's shenanigans—the thought of food was nauseating.

Surprisingly, Maggie nodded. "I'm starving," she said as she pushed up from the sofa. "But let's go out. It's our day off and neither one of us should be cooking."

I couldn't argue with that.

I WALKED WALLY AS promised while Maggie got ready, then I drove us to our favorite diner in Floydsville. After breakfast, we took a leisurely drive down the coast, though it wasn't as pleasant as I'd hoped, thanks to all the tourist traffic. It was a good thing I was driving, because Maggie had a tendency to get a bit... aggressive.

Rather than the relaxing drive I'd hoped for, I was a bundle of nerves by the time I headed back north toward Crown Hill. But it was such a nice day, I hated to go home. Instead, I made a circuit of the town while we listened to the oldies station. Maggie preferred disco, of all things, while I liked jazz. Oldies was a compromise.

Normally, Maggie belted out the wrong lyrics to the songs, but she was being quiet. Too quiet.

Allen's death was in the forefront of my mind, though I kept my thoughts to myself. I certainly didn't want to bring up that traumatic event. But I mulled things over in my head. Especially the fact that I thought Edwin Evans might be a prime suspect.

I was so lost in my thoughts, I startled when Maggie broke the silence. "Look, Victor's at the funeral home," she said, pointing toward the parking lot. I hadn't even realized I'd been driving by the place.

"We should go say hi," she suggested. I gave her a puzzled look at the suggestion, but I turned into the lot nonetheless. Thankfully, since I'd started dating Robert, Maggie had quit teasing me for being attracted to Victor. Of all the silly things she'd come up with, that one was pretty close to the top of the list.

The sign on the window stated the place was closed Sundays, but the door was unlocked.

"Hello?" I called as we stepped inside the lobby. "Victor? Are you here?"

"Back room," came a muffled voice over a speaker. I realized then that they must have had some sort of security system with intercoms.

I knew from having gone to the funeral home before when we'd been secretly investigating the Fishhook Killer's murders that there were hidden doors in the paneling, so Maggie and I walked up to one, and pressed on the wall until a section

64

opened up.

"That's just weird," I mumbled, though I was sure I'd said much the same before. Having hidden doors in a creepy place like a funeral parlor was just too much like the horror movies Maggie liked.

We passed through the coffin room, which was really creepy with the lights off, lit only thanks to the autopsy room's door being opened.

"I always expect someone to sit up in one of those," Maggie whispered, pointing toward the coffins.

"They're empty," I reminded her. "Just for show."

"I know, but still." Frankly, I had to agree, even though I kept it to myself, and we both hurried through the room.

Victor was wearing the same type of gown I'd seen countless times on television detective shows, the blue type the coroner wore. I noticed he'd covered the body he was obviously working on, which I was thankful for.

"What are you two ladies doing here?" he asked. Victor was creepy, but mostly just his looks. So far, he'd been nothing but nice to us, despite his Bela Lugosi appearance.

I tried my best to smile pleasantly, but it was difficult considering our surroundings. Two bodies on steel tables under sheets within spitting distance was a bit unnerving.

"We were just driving—"

"Did you get Allen Rogers' body yet?" Maggie interrupted. The abrupt question startled me, and from the look on his face, Victor as well. I was a bit shocked she would even ask the question.

"If you mean the, ehm, burn victim, then yes," Victor admitted as he motioned to the table closest to us. I had to admit that a part of me wanted to pull the sheet down to see what a burned corpse looked like, but then I realized that no, I really didn't want to know. Poor Maggie, though.

"Did you find out what the cause of death was?" Maggie said in a rather demanding way as she crossed her arms over her chest. I frowned at my friend.

Who are you? She was certainly acting out of character.

Victor seemed to agree, as he blinked a few times, a frown crinkling his brow. "Well, the cause of death was rather obvious."

"Was it?" Maggie asked, somewhat haughtily.

Victor's frown deepened. "Well, yes, it's apparent the victim was burned to death."

"So that's your final report?" she asked as she lifted her chin. Victor looked like he was going to start squirming.

He shook his head. "I really shouldn't be discussing—"

"Did you run a toxicology scan? Get x-rays? Check for wounds?"

Victor glanced at me, and I just shrugged, wide-eyed. *No idea*, I mouthed. He looked back at Maggie.

"I can't talk about the case," he told her gently. I wondered if he'd realized she was a bit unhinged. "It's under investigation, although it does appear to be simply an accident."

"Well, appearances can be deceiving," Maggie told him. "You shouldn't make assumptions." She spun on her heel and marched out of the room, leaving both Victor and I staring after her with open mouths. After a few seconds, I glanced back at him.

"Sorry. She, uh, was a bit attached to Allen Rogers. I guess it's making her sort of…"

"Pushy?" Victor supplied with a half-laugh.

I nodded. "Yeah, I guess so."

He rubbed his jaw with his gloved hand, making me wince as I wondered what all he'd been touching with it.

"Well, maybe she's right," he said as he side-eyed me. "The police seemed to think it was just an accident, that the victim had unintentionally burned himself up, but…" His voice trailed off and I stared at him.

"But?" I prompted.

He sighed. "I shouldn't be telling you this," he repeated as he motioned to the closest covered body, "but I have suspicions that Mr. Rogers was in an accident."

"Accident? You mean, other than being burned?"

Victor nodded. "Yeah." He pursed his lips for a moment. "I think I do need to get some x-rays." He turned back to the table and started to pull the sheet back.

"And that's my cue to leave," I said as I spun around and chased after Maggie.

Chapter 7

I WAS A BIT concerned about Maggie. For one thing, she was uncharacteristically quiet. For another, when she did break that silence, she wasn't her usual self. In fact, she was rather... articulate.

It was scary.

"So," I said with a wary glance toward my friend as I drove us back toward our end of town, "is there anything else you want to do? Anywhere else you want to go?" I secretly chanted *Please say no, please say no.*

"I want to go back to the cabin," she said, her voice sounding flat.

"The cabin?" I asked, not because I didn't know where she meant, but because I was a little shocked that she'd want to return to the scene of the crime. Or the accident, if Jonny was to be believed.

Maggie didn't answer as she stared out the window. I sighed, but I headed toward the mountain.

Of course, I had no idea where we were going, exactly. I knew where the main road that led up the mountain was, but after that, I really had no idea.

It seemed like we had driven for an hour, though I knew it was more likely about half that. I scanned the trees lining the side of the road, watching for a break signaling the goat path road leading to the cabin.

"Look out!"

I jerked my eyes back to the road in front of us, then swerved, narrowly avoiding a bicyclist. I remembered then Robert mentioning that the area had been a bad one for pedestrians and cyclists. I could see why.

The man gave us the finger as we drove by.

Maggie rolled down her window and returned the gesture.

"Good luck to you, too!" she yelled, while I rolled my eyes. No matter how many times I told her that the middle finger wasn't a "Hawaiian good luck sign," she insisted on using it. One of these days, she was going to get us shot.

We drove another few miles when I thought I should turn around and head back to town, but Maggie pointed.

"There," she said.

I squinted through the dark woods and saw what she was pointing at; it was a break in the tree line, possibly a road. Even though there was no one else around–except for an angry cyclist miles back–I signaled to turn.

It didn't take long to realize we weren't on the right road, but I couldn't turn around. I hoped whoever lived at the end of the lane wouldn't be too upset when my old Buick pulled up to their front door.

After a few moments, the tree line broke into a meadow, much like the one we'd seen the evening before at Allen's cabin. In fact, the cabin that came into view looked just like Allen's, minus the decorative well out front.

"Do you think this is Todd's cabin?" I asked, though Maggie didn't answer. I glanced at her, just to see if she was awake. She was, and was just staring out the window at the little log cabin before us.

I was starting to really worry about her.

Looking around, I didn't see Todd's truck, though there was a small SUV parked on the side of the cabin. I debated for a moment what to do, if we should turn around, or maybe knock on the door and ask directions. Before I could decide, Maggie opened her door and got out, then marched toward the front door.

She knocked before I'd even gotten my door open. In just seconds, the door opened… along with my mouth.

Edwin Evans in the flesh!

I fumbled with my door handle, trying to exit the vehicle before Maggie said something stupid to tick the man off. It took several tries in my excitement, but I finally managed the amazing feat of opening the car door, then hurried toward the little porch.

"…I have no idea," Edwin was telling Maggie. He had a sour look on his face, and I wondered what she'd already said to anger the man. He glanced my way.

"Great, a silver fox invasion."

Despite his rude words, I smiled broadly. "Hello, Mr. Evans," I said pleasantly, though my voice shook a little. "I recognize you from the back of your books. I have all of them. Your books, I mean. You're one of my favorite authors."

I knew I was gushing and sounded a bit like a schoolgirl meeting a Hollywood heartthrob, but I couldn't seem to help myself. Maggie even glanced my way, a confused look on her face.

"Yeah, yeah," Edwin muttered. "What is it you want?"

I blinked a few times at the snarliness and a part of me wondered if Allen had been right about the man, that he was just surly and rude.

"I have a book to finish, so out with it."

"Oh," I breathed, "is it the next book in *The Dead of the Night* series? That's been my favorite series of yours so far."

That earned me a look that led me to believe he was about to slam the door in our faces.

"We're trying to find Allen Rogers' cabin," I hurried on. "We need to—"

"Yeah, yeah," the man waved, then thumbed toward Maggie. "Already told this one that I don't know where that moron is staying. I'm still perturbed that he followed me up here in the first place. Up to no good, I'm telling you."

I was surprised at that. Allen had made it seem like a coincidence that the two authors had ended up in the same place, but the more I thought about it, the more ridiculous that was. Crown Hill was certainly no huge tourist destination, even though we did garner quite a few beach-goers, but those were

70

mostly from the surrounding area. From what I knew, Edwin Evans lived in Albany, New York, some three hundred miles away. It made me wonder how Allen knew where Edwin would be.

Edwin pointed his finger at Maggie. "When you find that idiot, you tell him—"

"He's dead," she said flatly, interrupting the tirade.

The shock on Edwin's face seemed genuine, and I felt instant relief in knowing it was very unlikely the man had had anything to do with Allen's death.

"How? Car accident?" he asked, recovering from his shock as his face morphed back into a scowl. I wondered if that was his usual expression. Resting grump face.

"No," I shook my head, figuring I should answer so Maggie didn't have to relive the trauma. "He was... well, the police and coroner think it was an accident, but he was, um, burned in his cabin," I said, motioning toward the south, the general direction of Allen's cabin.

"Burned?" Edwin asked, his frown deepening. "Didn't see fire or smoke, or hear any fire trucks."

Maggie and I both shook our heads. "The cabin didn't burn," she said. "Just... him."

The man looked between the two of us. "How is that possible?"

I nodded. "I know, I had the same question. But Todd—your, uh, landlord—"

He waved, "Yeah, yeah, I know who Todd Evans is. And he's no relation, mind you."

I smiled. "We know, he already told us. Anyway, Todd said the cabins are constructed mostly of laminate wood, which doesn't burn. So even though Allen..."

I let my voice trail off as I glanced at Maggie. She looked a bit paler than normal, but she seemed to be holding it together. This "new" Maggie was a bit disconcerting and I would admit only to myself that I missed the goofy, see-a-monster-around-

71

every-corner version.

"Hmm," Edwin said as he ran his finger along his top lip. It was then I noticed he held a cigar in his hand. My lip curled in distaste before I could stop it, but I also saw that it wasn't lit.

"Might have to use that in the book," he said, obviously to himself. He seemed to remember we were still standing on his porch, because he shook his head slightly, then reached back to grab the door. "If you ladies don't mind, I have a book to get back to."

"Oh, of course, Mister Evans," I said as I grabbed Maggie's arm and pulled her back. She didn't resist as we backed off the porch. "Happy writing!" I said with a wave. My sentiment was met with a door slam.

"Rude man," Maggie muttered as we walked back to the car.

I felt the need to defend him, for some reason, though I knew if it had been anyone else, I would have been saying the same thing.

"He's busy," I protested as we reached the car. Once we were inside, I continued. "Can't really blame him for wanting to get back to his work."

I started the car, then turned around in the meadow, though it took three tries, since my old Buick was so long. "I really need to get a smaller car," I griped once we were heading back down the small path to the main road.

"Well, at least we know which direction to go," I said as I turned left to head back the way we'd come. "Watch out for the turn-off."

It took two tries—and multiple attempts to turn around again—before we found the path leading to Allen's cabin. "I have no idea how Robert found that so easily last night," I muttered.

"He was a cop," Maggie said with a shrug. "He's more observant than most people."

I nodded, though I didn't really agree. I always prided myself on being very observant.

Todd's truck was in the front of the cabin, the front door open. He came out and walked to his truck before he noticed us. He smiled as he pulled those little headphone things out of his ears.

"Hi, ladies!" he called out with a wave. We got out of the car and walked up to him. Todd gave us both a hug, which was his usual greeting. I realized that he hadn't hugged us the night before, but it was understandable, considering the circumstances.

"What are you doing here?" he asked. I shrugged.

"Well, we just, uh…" I really had no idea what to say. We hadn't planned it out. How to explain that we wanted to nose around the cabin and see if we could find any evidence of foul play made us sound a bit loony.

"We're curious about how Allen died," Maggie said. I whipped my head toward her and widened my eyes, a *Why are you admitting that?* look on my face.

Todd laughed, though it wasn't a very humorous sound… again, likely thanks to the circumstances. He tugged on a toolbox in the bed of his truck and opened it.

"Well, considering the cops just wrote it off as an accident without even poking around, I gotta say I'm glad someone is interested." He pulled a prybar out of his toolbox, then turned toward the cabin. We followed.

"I contacted the company where I buy all my laminate," Todd said as he walked toward the bedroom. I was surprised Maggie followed. I truly expected her to have a meltdown once we were inside. I'd been prepared for it, knowing I'd have to haul her out. But she had a ramrod stiff spine as she marched behind the man and didn't even hesitate to follow him into the bedroom.

"Told them their product was amazing," Todd's voice floated down the short hall while I looked around the living room. "Saved the cabin, and who knows, maybe even the whole mountain, from burning."

There was some banging and the sound of something being

ripped up—presumably the flooring, while Todd continued telling Maggie how he'd sent pictures of the floor and wall.

I looked around the area, noting that it looked the same as it had the night before. Apparently, Jonny hadn't done any investigation at all. Even Allen's laptop was still on the coffee table. The deconstruction noises continued, so I stepped over to the table and sunk down on the couch.

Even though Jonny hadn't seemed interested in investigating the death, I knew there was a possibility that could change, so I used the hem of my blouse to pick up the computer, careful not to leave my fingerprints on it. The last thing I needed was for Jonny to think I'd had something to do with Allen's death... or Allen himself. He'd already had a suspicion along those lines, the idiot.

I wasn't too great with computers but knew enough to at least turn it on. The screen flashed almost immediately when I hit the button with the circle and a line through it. Like with Robert's laptop and the computer Elle had purchased for us at the bakery, I'd expected a password screen to greet me, and had prepared for the disappointment of that, but instead, it opened to a browser window.

"That's not very smart," I muttered. Anyone could have gotten a hold of his computer and gotten into his files. Even I knew that.

I frowned when I saw Allen had been looking at Edwin's website. It was open to the "About Me" page. The page was paused where it mentioned Edwin's military history. He'd served two tours in the Gulf with the Army during the Iraqi crisis, which I knew. A sentence was highlighted—Evans was a fire control specialist, which I knew, though I frowned; that was a strange thing to focus on.

There were other tabs at the top of the window and I clicked one. It was a lawyer's site entitled "Terrorist Threat Laws and Penalties." The page was stopped on a section detailing what constituted such a threat.

I clicked on the last tab and was surprised to see the Crown Hill Police Department's website. It was their "contact us" page, stopped at Chief Richard Thompson's info. "Why would he want to talk to Dickie?" I wondered out loud.

Clicking on the line that minimized the browser window, I looked for other things he had opened. One was a white circle with an "S" in the middle and I clicked on it. It opened what appeared to be some sort of writing software program and my confused frown deepened when I read what Allen had been writing. The last sentence caught my eye.

"The fire marshal's report detailed the death: The victim had been inside the bedroom when his house burned down. The body was burned beyond recognition, a charcoal briquette. It was obviously arson... and murder."

"Well, that's not the best writing, is it? In fact, it's pretty lousy." I mumbled, even as I chewed my lip in consideration of the fact that Allen had possibly written his own death. A premonition? I shook my head. That was highly unlikely, though it was strange.

The left-hand side of the program had a column with chapter headings, so I clicked on the previous one. It was more bad writing—making me glad I'd never spent money on any of Allen's books—and I had to force myself to read through some of it.

"...wondering if he should move on, Cross considered what he would lose. His deposit. The rest of the month's rent. The friends he'd made in the area. But worst of all, his mojo."

"Ugh, that's horrible," I griped. I started to read further, but Todd's voice interrupted me.

"I need to get some new planks," he told Maggie. "Not to sound rude, but I need to lock the place up."

I slammed the laptop closed and stood, making a move to head back to the front door, but something on the floor near the table leg caught my eye. I bent down to get a closer look, readjusting my glasses as I did so. My eyes widened when my sight adjusted and I could make out what the dark, nickel-sized thing was.

A cigar ash.

Chapter 8

I WAS THANKFUL for Maggie's distractedness as we headed back down the mountain. I was too wrapped up in my own thoughts to try to make small talk.

Or any talk, for that matter.

After seeing that cigar ash, I started looking around the cabin more thoroughly. Without going into the bedroom—which I really wanted to do but couldn't think of any good reason to give Todd—I quickly examined the area while Maggie and Todd talked.

There were several other strange things that most people wouldn't have noticed, but since I had a little bit of pre-knowledge about Allen, they caught my eye.

For one, the bag of coffee he'd bought was in the trash next to the kitchen counter. Knowing how much Allen loved that Sumatra coffee, it was certainly strange to see the package hadn't been opened.

I thought for a moment that maybe he'd died right after buying it, but then remembered Todd saying he'd seen the man just two nights before. So, if he'd made it a point to drive all the way down the mountain, across Crown Hill and into the downtown area to where the bakery was—dealing with tourist traffic along the way—just to get a cup of the stuff twice a day, why would he buy the coffee and then not make it? And why throw it away? What a waste of money. That coffee wasn't cheap.

Also, there was a book on the small dining table next to a single key, which I assumed was for the cabin. The book wouldn't have been noteworthy, except it was one of Edwin's books. As we walked to the front door, I reached out and flipped the cover up, seeing an inscription:

Hope you enjoy reading the book as much as I enjoyed writing it.

That also wasn't too unusual; after all, the men were contemporaries and I figured authors would read other works in their own genre. But it was unusual in that Edwin, who obviously didn't like Allen, would sign a book for him.

It was really strange, though, that the book was on the dining table. The body was found in the bedroom, on the window seat. In my experience, that was the perfect place to curl up with a book. The only time I'd done any reading at a table was when I'd been doing homework back in the day. Pleasure reading was meant to be done in comfortable places, not in a hardwood dining chair.

I supposed that the "clues"—if they could be called that—weren't unusual in and of themselves, but together they seemed to be obviously pointing to Edwin.

It was the "obvious" part that got to me. "I think I watch too many conspiracy shows," I murmured.

"What?" Maggie asked. I startled; she'd been so quiet I'd nearly forgotten she was in the car with me.

"Oh, nothing," I told her. I glanced her way; she was still just staring out the window, a blank look on her face.

"Do you want to go to Kirby's?" I asked, though it was done reluctantly. Kirby's crabcake sandwiches gave Maggie terrible gas, but it was her favorite place to eat. And I was willing to try anything to get her out of her funk, even if it meant having to wear a gasmask.

She turned to look at me. "We just ate two hours ago," she said as she motioned to the car stereo's clock, then shrugged. "Sure."

Being late Sunday afternoon, Kirby's was mostly empty, and we were able to get our favorite table by the window overlooking the north beach. Families were still enjoying the day, red-skinned, worn-out looking parents chasing after kids who seemed to be made completely of energy and enthusiasm. I didn't miss those days, to be honest. There was something to be said about being older. Less responsibility, for one. More rest and less noise, for another.

"I envy them," Maggie said softly, drawing my attention.

"Who?" I asked as I sipped my iced tea. Plain, just the way I liked it. Maggie liked hers with so much sugar in it, the spoon could stand straight up. She said "sweet tea" was the thing she missed the most after moving from the south.

She motioned toward the window, to the beachgoers. "The kids," she sighed. "Must be nice to just play all day, no cares, no worries."

I nodded, though she was still staring out the window and not looking at me. While I agreed with Maggie, a part of me also wanted to point out that she herself had few responsibilities. I took care of the household bills—she paid half the utilities, but I told her how much they were—and I handled all the bakery's business. Well, I did, before Elle came and took that part over, for which I'll always be grateful. All Maggie had to worry about was baking.

"I think I'd rather be one of your cats," I chuckled. "They don't have to do anything at all, just lay around, scratch the furniture and shed their fur. Kids still have to worry about going to school come autumn."

My comment drew a smile, at least. Maggie glanced my way, then took a sip of her tea. She winced, then added two more packets of sugar. My back teeth ached just watching her. She already had a pile of empty packets next to her glass.

"Wally has it pretty good, too," she said. "He sleeps all day, goes outside whenever he wants, and gets belly rubs and ear scratches on demand."

I chuckled. Rosie brought our food over then and we fussed over our plates, adding ketchup and salt to the fries, though Maggie liked pepper on hers. It was akin to french fry blasphemy, if you asked me.

By unspoken agreement, we held hands to ask a blessing over the food, then dug in. The sandwiches were delicious, as always. I'd tried for years to get Roland to give me the recipe, but he'd laughingly said his dad—the famous Kirby—would crawl out of his grave and strangle him.

We both only ate half our food since it hadn't been that long since we'd stuffed our faces at the diner in Floydsville, so we got to-go boxes and then decided to walk along the beach. I think neither one of us really wanted to go back home, back to reality.

Though the beach was still occupied by fun-seekers, it was relatively quiet, which I appreciated. The last thing I wanted, or needed, was a bunch of squawking kids and bellowing parents. My brain was in enough turmoil.

"It's crazy," Maggie said as we stood side-by-side, staring at the waves rolling in, leaving rivulets of water as it ran back out. The sea had always been mesmerizing to me, almost hypnotic.

"What is?" I asked as I glanced at her. Maggie's shoulders lifted.

"Sorry, I was just talking out loud."

I snorted. "Well, most talking is out loud," I laughed. She looked at me with a confused look and I waved my hand.

"Never mind. Do you want to tell me what you were thinking?"

Maggie looked back out over the waves. "I was just thinking that it's funny how history repeats itself."

My eyes widened. Maggie didn't usually have anything too deep—or intelligent, for that matter–to say. And that wasn't being unkind, just truthful. "What do you mean?"

She glanced my way again. "I... I was thinking about last night. About Allen," she sighed. "About how we... how we found him," she whispered. She looked away, but not before I saw the tears glistening in her eyes.

"I know you had gotten close to the guy," I said as I wrapped my arm around her shoulders. I hated to voice that out loud, but I didn't know what else to say to comfort her. She barely knew the guy, but she seemed to be grieving him far more than I would have thought was necessary for someone she'd just met.

Maggie surprised me by shaking her head. "That's not what I mean," she murmured. I had to tilt my head closer to her to hear what she was saying, especially with the ocean so close.

"When I moved here from Georgia, I never told you why." Her shoulders stiffened and I released her. She turned toward me.

"The same thing happened back home," she said as a lone tear tracked down her cheek. She absently wiped at it.

I stared at her in shock. "You found a burned body?" It was insane to think that the same thing would have happened to her twice in one lifetime.

She shook her head. "No, I mean I... another man I l-loved was m-murdered," she stammered.

I couldn't stop my mouth from dropping open. Not because she thought of Allen as someone she "loved"—well, there was that—but the rest of it was more shocking.

"What?" I said far too loudly. "You never told me that!"

Maggie sighed again, her shoulders drooping. "I couldn't. I just... I couldn't talk about it."

I nodded, though I was still a bit hurt by the fact that the person I thought was my best friend had kept something so incredible from me.

"Juan Carlo was so wonderful," Maggie whispered. At least, I think that's what she said. I leaned closer again when she stared at the sand between us.

"He was so handsome," she went on. "Tall, exotic, prettier than a man should be. But he was also kindhearted. Everyone just loved him. Including me."

My heart went out to her and I put my hand on her arm. "I'm so sorry, honey," I said. I couldn't imagine what she'd gone through. And I didn't want to. My mind rejected even the mere thought of Robert...

I shuddered.

Though I wanted to ask details about how Juan Carlo was

murdered, it was obviously poor form, so I just rubbed her arm in what I hoped was consolation. I didn't have to ask, though, when Maggie went on.

"His girlfriend found out he was cheating on her," she sniffed.

"With you?" That came out in a bit of a screech, and I cleared my throat.

Maggie shook her head. "No, with his receptionist." I frowned, wondering what kind of a man this was, if he was seeing both Maggie and his receptionist. I also wondered just how old he was, as Maggie had to be in her sixties then, since she'd moved to Crown Hill ten years prior.

"Gina read a text message the receptionist sent," Maggie went on. "She went to the office and..." Her voice trailed off and she looked at me, her eyes filling once again.

"Gina shot Juan Carlo right in the middle of an appointment."

I think my mouth dropped open even more, even as I wondered what type of appointment she was talking about. "You're kidding," I breathed. "That's horrible!"

Maggie nodded. "I know. It was so awful."

"I bet," I agreed, trying to sympathize, though it was difficult with realizing Maggie had been in love with a two-timing cheater. I tried to think of something else to say, how to ask about the relationship, but Maggie beat me to it.

"The worst part was not getting to see him every week," she sniffled. "Once Juan Carlo was gone, everything just fell apart."

I made a sympathetic noise. At least, I hoped it sounded that way. "You said you loved him."

She nodded so vigorously, her curls bobbed. "I did. He was just so wonderful," she said dreamily.

A little boy screamed then, making us jump. We turned to watch as he ran from the incoming surf like it was hot lava. Though I could do without the screaming, it was nice to watch the child having so much fun. Especially after all the ugliness from the past day.

I turned to Maggie again. "Look, I don't want to poke my finger in the wound, but how is it you loved this Juan person if he was a cheater?" I tilted my head to the side. "Seems to me that's a strange sort of relationship."

A tiny, confused frown appeared between her brows. "That didn't matter," she said, surprising me. "None of his women cared about that."

I stared at her for a moment. "None of his women? Just how many girlfriends did this man have?"

She shook her head. "Just one," she said, her frown deepening. "Well, and his receptionist."

I was getting more confused by the second. "So, you mean this Juan Carlo person wasn't your boyfriend?"

Maggie laughed, though it wasn't a humorous sound. "Heavens no! He was my hairdresser. A real genius with curly hair," she added as she patted her hair.

My fingers flexed several times, and my face must have reflected my thoughts, because the screaming little boy looked our way, got a horrified look on his face, and went running for his father.

There were times–a lot of them, actually–when I really, really wanted to choke the woman.

Chapter 9

IF I NEVER SAW another cupcake in all my days, I'd be thrilled. After a local youth football team called the bakery and ordered twenty-three dozen cupcakes for their upcoming banquet, it was all hands on deck to get the order out. All but Elle, who was just too tired.

I was beginning to worry about my daughter, if she might be falling into depression.

One good thing came out of the cupcake order—besides the money it generated—we discovered that Jasmin is fabulous at cake decorating, something none of us excelled at. Maggie was a wonderful baker, but her decorating skills were pretty basic. Mine were mostly non-existent. But Jasmin had a real knack for it, which she probably got from her artist father.

"You're good enough to make wedding cakes!" Maggie exclaimed when Jasmin showed her a cupcake she'd decorated with butterflies. I'd laughed at it, thinking it wasn't exactly up to footballer standards, but she'd been experimenting with the different design tips.

"I don't know about that," Jasmin said, though she had a satisfied grin. It made me happy to see my granddaughter seeming to find a place for herself. She was amazing with the customers—admitting she'd held waitressing jobs through college—and seemed to have a keen sense of what needed to be done and when. She'd often jump in and handle something before Maggie and I even noticed it needed doing.

Since Maggie and I had prayed for help just moments before Elle and Jasmin walked in our door, I knew they were really and truly a "godsend."

"You should look at some videos on decorating," Maggie went on. "I bet you could figure it out really fast." I nodded in agreement, though I had no idea there were such videos.

Robert brought a tray of cupcakes from the back room

where they'd been cooling. We all had to stay long after closing to get the order out, and I was glad it had come when it did, because keeping Maggie so busy was certainly helping her get out of her funk.

Normally, I got angry with my friend for dwelling on things because most of the time, they were ridiculous. I'd never forget the time she'd lost a good week's sleep because she'd convinced herself that aliens had gotten into her house through the basement and were implanting bugs in her ears when she slept.

"I keep seeing worms!" she'd cried. I had tried to convince her that they were called "floaters" and that a lot of people had them, but she'd been adamant that she had bugs in her head. I'd started calling her Maggie Maggot, just to try to tease her out of it, but it wasn't until she'd gone to the eye doctor and he'd told her the same thing about the floaters that I had, that she'd relented.

But now, I was trying to be considerate of Maggie's feelings. Even though it would be a bit silly to be pining after a man she'd barely known a week, I understood how traumatic it must have been to see his body in the condition it had been found. I understood it, but I couldn't fathom how horrible it must have been.

Jasmin laughed at something Maggie said that I didn't catch, drawing me out of my thoughts. "Well, despite how beautiful those butterflies are," I said as I pointed a pastry bag at my granddaughter, "we need to concentrate on getting these more childish and boyish cupcakes out first. You can work on your frilly skills later."

Jasmin grinned at me as she picked up her own pastry bag and started filling the tops of the little cakes with mocha frosting. "Isn't that redundant?" she asked as she covertly winked at me with a slight head nod Robert's way.

"Is what redundant?" I asked, playing along.

Her grin widened. "Childish and boyish. Aren't all males childish?"

"Hey, now," Robert fake-growled at her, making Jasmin

laugh. He yanked a towel off the counter and started twirling it in a threatening manner.

Jasmin's laugh turned to a cackle. "If you whack me with that, I swear I'm gonna decorate you prettier than that cupcake. But I'll use a permanent marker to do it. You'll be adorable with unicorns and hearts all over your face."

Robert's lips twitched, but he didn't stop spinning the towel between his hands. "Worth it," he said, then took a step toward her. Jasmin shrieked and dashed behind me, peeking out at the man from over my shoulder.

"That's not fair," Robert said, his bottom lip sticking out in a pout to rival any Maggie had ever given. "I can't hit a woman."

Behind me, I felt Jasmin stiffen. I knew what she was thinking... about her father and how Carl had been abusive toward her mother. Elle still hadn't opened up to me about the situation, but Jasmin had shared a little.

I still wanted to pay the man a visit.

"And what am I?" Jasmin said with a chuckle, though it sounded a bit forced. My heart went out to her.

"You're just a girl," Robert shrugged, unaware of the unease he'd just inadvertently caused. I hadn't told him about Carl... but I was going to. I planned on taking my man with me when I paid that creep a visit. He had a firearm, after all.

"A mere child," Robert went on. "And the Bible says, 'spareth not the rod in beating thy child'."

I laughed at his terrible misquote and he grinned back at me. I'd managed to talk Robert into attending church with us, though he'd grown up in a different faith. I was thankful he found our little church "refreshing," without all the rules, traditions and obligations he'd had at his former church that had driven him away years before.

It hurt to think how close I'd come to being driven away from my own church—though it was completely of my own doing. Things had been so much better, though, once I dropped out of most all the committees and ministries I'd been a part of.

I'd been a bit surprised at how easily Pastor and Betty had found others to fill the roles I'd once held, and I had a bit of guilt for "hogging" all the ministry opportunities. At the time I'd taken on so many duties, I think I'd been trying to keep very active to avoid grieving Frank so much. But then it just became rote to continue working for the church. And that was exactly what I had been doing... working for the church and not the Lord.

"Well, I'm not a child," Jasmin said as she leaned around me to stick her tongue out at Robert. He responded by pretending to whip the towel toward her, making her shriek again.

"Lands' sake!" I cried, though it was with a laugh. I cupped my ear and shook my head. "You still scream like you did when you were five," I chastised my granddaughter as I glanced over my shoulder. Then I turned and pointed at Robert and the towel in his hand.

"And you... you're proving the 'males are childish' statement."

He responded with more pouting as he put the towel back on the counter. "Every party needs a pooper, that's why we invited you, party pooper... party pooperrr," he sang quietly. I might have been losing my hearing, but I still caught it and slung a dollop of vanilla frosting at him that hit him square in the chest. Everyone laughed.

I was glad for the good-natured camaraderie, especially when we were so swamped with orders. The football banquet was the biggest one, but we also had several donut orders to fill for nearby businesses, along with a French pastry sampler for a high tea at the country club.

Laughing and joking around did much to get my mind off of... well, everything. It had been four days since we'd discovered Allen's body and I was constantly mulling over the how's and why's of the death. So far, I hadn't come up with anything useful, but Maggie and I had decided we were going to make another trip to the cabin to see if we could find anything else noteworthy.

The chime rang and we all looked up, ready to tell whoever it was that we were closed. Despite the big sign on the door that indicated we were closed, people still tried the handle, which was unlocked so James could come and go easily, and we wouldn't have to stop what we were doing to let him in and out.

Jasmin had made the excellent suggestion of hiring a delivery driver, paying them via a delivery charge and whatever tips they received. It was no money out of our pocket but brought in extra sales from those who couldn't get out to pick up their order. Elle said our sales had increased eighteen percent in the past few days since we'd added delivery and James was making excellent money before and after school hours. I still couldn't believe the kid managed to get all over town on just an old Vespa.

"Back already?" Jasmin asked. James got the same shocked look he always did whenever Jasmin talked to him, and Robert elbowed me. We'd been talking about the huge crush the boy had on my granddaughter earlier. I'd denied it, but Robert had insisted. Judging by the way the teen's face flamed just then, I'd have to admit Robert was right.

"We have another delivery," Maggie said, drawing the kid's pretty blue eyes back to the others in the room. Maggie pulled a box out of the cooler and set it on the display case.

"This one goes to Mason's."

James looked confused. "The grocery store?"

Maggie nodded. "Yep," she grinned. "They're having a birthday party for the manager and wanted a good cake. Not like the cruddy ones they make."

We offered cakes, though only with very basic decorations. But considering we'd already had three different requests for wedding cakes in the few short weeks we'd been opened, I thought pushing Jasmin to learn the art was not a bad idea at all.

"Good thing the scooter has a luggage bag," James said with a crooked grin as he slid the cake across the glass top. He really was a handsome young man. It was a shame he was too young for Jasmin. They would have made an adorable couple.

"I'd wanted the motocross bike old man Charlie had for sale, but when I got there, he said it'd been stolen last Friday." James shrugged. "Got the Vespa instead that had been used as a courier bike just cuz I was desperate for a ride. But then I got the job here." He grinned again as he glanced at Jasmin with doe eyes.

"Maybe it was fate."

Robert elbowed me again thanks to the schmoozy moment, further rubbing it in that he was right. I frowned at him, but he was looking at James.

"Old man Charlie... you mean Charlie Franchetti?" James nodded, and Robert said, "Hmm, interesting," but didn't elaborate. I made a mental note to ask him later.

Once James was off with the last delivery for the night, Robert locked the front door and we got busy cranking out cupcakes and the French pastries for the country club tea scheduled the following day. We worked until the sun went down, then all groaned over our aching backs, necks and hands from squeezing pastry bags as we headed home.

"I think we need more help in the bakery," Maggie moaned from the backseat of Robert's truck. I turned toward her, wincing when a muscle in my back protested.

"I agree, but let's have Jasmin do the hiring," I said with a nod toward my granddaughter. "She did such a good job hiring James, I think it's yet another forte of hers."

Jasmin's mouth scrunched to the side. "Yeah," she drawled, "because I hired the one and only kid willing to work basically on commission and not hourly, I have a future in human resources. Go, me."

I laughed at her sassiness, something I never would have tolerated in her mother. There was certainly something to be said for grandchildren—they could get away with just about anything.

"She'll just hire another babe magnet like James," Robert

quipped, grinning at Jasmin through the rearview mirror. She rolled her eyes at him, though her lips twitched as she fought a smile.

"Babe magnet?" I asked, eyebrows raised. He grinned.

"That's a good-looking man who attracts women," Maggie said. I glanced at her.

"Really," I said drolly.

She nodded with enthusiasm, like she was imparting great wisdom I wasn't aware of. "Yes, that's what it means. Babe, meaning girls, or females. And magnet, you know, like something that attracts."

"You don't say," I drawled. Jasmin cracked up and even Robert was fighting to keep his composure. "Regardless," I continued, "from now on, Jasmin can be our HR person."

"And the cake decorator," Maggie added.

Jasmin chortled. "Let's not forget counterperson, cashier, busser, coffee maker–"

"Chief cook and bottle washer," Robert added with a grin as he turned into our driveway.

"But I thought I was the chief cook," Maggie said. I wasn't looking at her, but I just knew she was pouting.

"Robert was just using an old expression for someone who does everything," I said as I reached for my door handle. Robert hissed at me, and I let go of it. He always insisted on opening the doors for us ladies. He let Jasmin out first since she was on his side.

"Hurry up, old man," I called as he walked around the front of the truck, Jasmin following. With the windows open, I know he heard me. It was confirmed by the gesture he gave me.

"Oh, Robert knows the Hawaiian good luck sign too!" Maggie squealed, while Jasmin clutched the hood of the truck in a fit of giggles.

"You guys are too much," my granddaughter told me as she hugged my arm to her. "I hope I can be half as fun as you are when I'm an old lady."

"You might not get to live that long if you keep mentioning the old part," I whispered to her as I motioned with my eyes toward Maggie. I'd warned Jasmin not to ever mention her age; Maggie was in perpetual age denial, and she had a wicked retaliatory pinch.

"They are fun, aren't they?" Maggie piped in. I eyeballed Jasmin, giving her a "See what I mean?" look. My granddaughter grinned.

Once we were inside, Jasmin headed to the bedroom to check on her mom while Maggie and I went into the kitchen to make popcorn and herbal tea, our nighttime ritual. Robert followed and sat at the kitchen table while we busied ourselves.

"What was the deal with Charlie Franchetti?" I asked him over my shoulder.

"What do you mean?"

I huffed; the man knew what I was hinting at, but I also knew he wanted me to spell it out. Frustrating creatures, men were.

"Why did you ask James for clarification about 'Old Man Charlie'?" I turned around and put my backside against the counter while crossing my arms and glaring at him. He responded with a cheeky grin.

"It was just interesting that James said Charlie's motorcycle had been stolen," he shrugged. I tipped my chin down and intensified my glare. That earned me a broader grin.

"Quit poking the bear!" I cried.

Maggie whirled around from where she'd been watching the popcorn, her hand over her heart. She gawked a bit frantically around the kitchen.

"A bear? Where?"

I gave her a look. "Do you really think we'd be having such a calm conversation if there was an actual bear standing here?" She had the sense to look a bit embarrassed, then turned back to the popcorn while I turned my attention back to Robert.

"James said the motorcycle had been stolen last Friday," he went on, "which was the day after the coroner said—" he glanced at Maggie with a wince. "The day after the, um, body had, uh, burned," he hedged. Maggie's shoulders stiffened, but she didn't comment.

"But the strange part is that Charlie lives just a half mile down the road from the, uh, cabin." He didn't need to specify which cabin.

"That is strange," I said as I tilted my head. "Are you going to tell Jonny?"

"You mean, Detective Jonathan Donovan?" Robert laughed. Jonny hated that I called him by his childhood name... which is the main reason I still did so.

"I'll call him when I get home. But I doubt he'll do much with the intel," he shrugged. "He's made up his mind it was just an accident."

I kept my suspicions about Edwin's involvement to myself.

Robert said his goodbyes then and we settled in to watch Law & Order. I was surprised when Jasmin joined us. Normally, the girl stayed in the room with her mother in the evenings. She was always on the computer and Elle had said Jasmin was trying to learn graphics design like her father, though she'd never gone to school for it. My granddaughter made me proud with her talents and ambitions.

"How's your mom?" Maggie asked before I could. Jasmin shrugged, not taking her eyes from the television as she helped herself to a handful of popcorn.

"She's still sleeping."

That was surprising; Elle had been sleeping most of the day. In fact, more times than not, that's what she was doing.

"Is she okay?" I asked. Jasmin glanced at me. "I mean, do you think she's depressed? Is that why she's sleeping so much?"

Jasmin started to say something, then shook her head. "No, that's not why." She grimaced. "I'd like to tell you all that's going on, but it's not my story. She'll tell you when she's ready, Gramma."

Well, that didn't help things one iota. All that statement had done was kick my curiosity further into gear. The next day was Maggie's and my half-day at the bakery, so I planned to spend some time with my daughter... and go to Allen's cabin again.

There was something about the whole thing that was bugging me, and I just couldn't put my finger on it. The Good Lord knew that Jonny wasn't going to investigate the death at all, the fool. I would have thought after the fiasco of the Fishhook Killer investigation he'd have learned his lesson about disregarding the possibilities of a crime taking place, even when the evidence seemed to point in other directions, but apparently not. Someone needed to investigate the death, but it obviously wasn't going to be the Crown Hill PD.

Which left it up to Maggie and me.

Chapter 10

MAGGIE INSISTED ON DRIVING to the cabin once we finished at the bakery, which was cause for a near nervous breakdown. The woman had no use for such mundane things as stop signs, stoplights, speed limits, or lane stripes.

I was sure my fingerprints were going to be permanently embedded in her dash by the time we pulled up to the cabin.

"I thought Todd would be here," Maggie whined as she put the car in park. Of course, she would be pouting; Todd was one of her frequent flirting victims.

"Well, I'm sure he finished the work he had to get done. The man is busy with lots of projects, you know."

Maggie nodded as we exited the vehicle. "You hit the nail with the head on that," she laughed, shaking her head. She didn't notice my pained smirk at her misuse of that particular idiom, because she was already marching toward the cabin.

"Todd has too many pans on fire," she added.

"Wow, two Maggieisms in as many seconds," I laughed.

"What was that?" she asked as she marched up the steps leading to the cabin's little porch.

"Nothing." There was no way I would be able to explain her mixed idioms. Knowing Maggie, she'd likely say something like, "Well, to each their own dose of medicine," or some such.

Maggie tried the doorknob, but it was locked. "Well, pooh," she muttered as she moved to the window. I wanted to tell her that, even if it was by chance unlocked, neither one of us was going to be able to fit our big booties through that small opening, but I left her to it as I stepped back and considered the situation.

Todd rents the cabin, I thought to myself. But I bet he doesn't meet each guest to give them a key, which means one is likely to be around here somewhere…

I stepped off the porch and headed around the side of the cabin, then around the back. It wasn't until I walked to the other side that I saw what I was looking for: right next to the electric meter was a lock box.

Lifting the outer lid on the box, I stared at the combination on the inner door. "Well, Todd, let's assume you use the same combo for everything," I muttered to myself as I inputted the combination Todd had used for the lock box he'd had at my house when he and his crew were doing the remodel.

It worked.

Grinning with my prize in hand, I hurried back to the front porch in time to see Maggie had managed to get the screen off the front window. "Never mind that," I told her as I held up the key, then unlocked the door.

Once inside, I headed straight to the bedroom, though I wasn't sure what I was going to find, especially since Todd had been working in the room, likely destroying any evidence that could have been left behind.

The room was dark, so I turned on the nightstand lamp and opened the blinds on the only window. Maggie stepped into the room then, surprising me. She nodded when she looked at the window seat, which looked perfectly normal to me. I could only imagine what it had looked like before... especially with the burned body on it.

An involuntary shudder coursed through me at the thought.

"I don't know what we're looking for," I told her as I planted my hands on my hips and stared at the floor. It was obvious where Todd had replaced the planks; they were darker and cleaner looking than the rest of the floor.

"Clues," Maggie murmured. I rolled my eyes.

"No kidding."

While she rummaged through the chest of drawers, I got down on my hands and knees and looked under the bed. It was too dark to see much, so I pulled my phone out of my back pocket and turned on the flashlight app. I'd had no idea the thing even had a flashlight, not until Elle showed me one day when I'd been trying to see in the back of the cabinet in the bakery's storeroom.

The whole underneath of the bed lit up thanks to the surprisingly bright light. "Handy inventions," I said of the cellphone. I'd never much cared for them and only had one for convenience, but I was starting to appreciate it more and more.

"What was that?" Maggie's voice, sounding muffled, called.

"Nothing," I answered as I adjusted my glasses to see better. There was something under the bed, near the center, but it was just out of reach. I flattened myself as best as a plump chesty woman could while on her belly and squeezed under the bed frame a little further as I stretched my fingers to grasp the object.

A screech from Maggie startled me so much, I banged my head on the bed above. "Ouch!" I griped as I shoved back out, then sat up on my knees to look over the bed at her. From the shriek she'd let out, I'd expected to see a costumed serial killer like from those stupid movies she liked, but there wasn't anything, or anyone.

"What's wrong?" I asked as I rubbed the back of my head. I was already getting a lump.

Maggie glanced at me over her shoulder. "Spider," she grimaced with a shudder as she continued going through a drawer, completely missing the glare I directed her way. I noticed the pile of clothing she was putting on the dresser top.

"You really think you're going to find clues in the man's underwear?"

She shrugged. "You never know. There might be something in here."

"Other than skid marks, I doubt it," I mumbled as I opened my hand to see what I'd found under the bed. I frowned; it was a ring. A man's wedding band, by the looks of it. I adjusted my glasses again and aimed my phone flashlight at the ring. There was an inscription.

J.T. —Forever and ever, amen. Brandy

"Okay," I muttered as I grabbed the mattress to pull myself to a stand. "That's not too helpful." I figured the ring had been lost by a former occupant of the cabin, and my mind went to the imaginings of an illicit tryst, wherein the ring's owner had taken it off to be with his lover, then lost the ring.

And, yes, I knew I was now jaded, thanks to finding out about Frank's affairs.

Tucking the ring in my pocket, I started to pull myself up, but noticed light shining out from under the bed, and realized it was my phone. When I lifted it, the light caught on something between the mattress and the bedframe. I frowned and started to reach for it, but had second thoughts.

"Hey, give me one of those drawers," I told Maggie. She turned to look at me in question, before turning back at the dresser. She grasped a drawer handle.

"Not those drawers!" I snapped as I waved my hand at the clothing pile. "A pair of underwear," I clarified. She frowned, then shrugged as she tossed a pair to me.

"These better be clean," I grumbled as I picked up the boxers with my finger and thumb, then used it as a glove to pull the object out.

"What did you find?" Maggie asked as she peered over the mattress.

I held it up. "A lighter." I didn't mention the ring. My thoughts were still a bit jumbled over my imaginings of a cheating husband.

Her eyes flickered toward the window seat and I could see the question in them. I was glad I'd had the foresight to keep my fingerprints off the thing; if it had been used to light Allen on fire, then we'd at least have the fingerprints of whoever it was who'd killed him.

My mind went back to Edwin and his cigars, though I kept my thoughts to myself.

Carefully tucking the lighter in the pocket with the ring, I stood and motioned toward the chest of drawers. "Put those clothes back and let's go check out his car." It was rather surprising that Allen's old Honda was still on the property, but I supposed Todd wasn't too worried about it since it was out of the way and as far as I knew, Allen didn't have any family who would want his possessions.

It was a sad thing to consider.

I locked the cabin and put the key back in the lock box before we walked across the meadow to where the car was tucked between the trees. It was rather strange that Allen would have parked so far away from the cabin, almost as if he'd been trying to hide his car from someone.

But who? And why?

"Whew, it's a trek out here, isn't it?" Maggie asked, fanning herself with her hand. The day was hot and humid, which was typical for our area in late spring and early summer. Whenever you got away from the beach and the cooling ocean breeze, you were subjected to a sauna-like atmosphere.

"And I thought Georgia was muggy," Maggie went on. I gave her a look; she said the same thing every single year when the temperatures soared.

It had been a little less than a week since we'd discovered Allen's body, but the car looked like it had been parked for a month. Leaves littered the top, bird droppings covered the glass and paint, and there was even a vine weed starting to grow through the back bumper.

"Todd said he'd seen Allen driving around just before..." I let my voice drift off, sorry that I'd brought up the death again. But that was ridiculous since we were at the cabin investigating it.

Maggie nodded as she bent to peer in the window. "Wow, it looks like he lived out of his car," she said. I looked over her shoulder; she wasn't kidding—the car was a disaster. Soda cans, fast food bags, to-go containers and candy wrappers littered the floor of the passenger side. In the back, cardboard boxes filled with books were strewn over the seat, with many loose copies on the floorboards. From what I could tell, they were all copies of the same book. Frowning, I looked a little closer and saw Allen's pen name on the cover.

"Looks like he was trying to sell his own books," I said as I straightened and examined the car again. It had the look of being abandoned.

"Is that blood?" Maggie asked and I looked where she was pointing at the back, near the trunk. I stepped closer and, sure enough, there was a dried stream of what certainly looked like blood on the back quarter panel, though it also had dripped down toward the back bumper. From the location, I would guess something bleeding was put in the trunk.

I got a chill then, despite the muggy heat.

"Should we open it?" Maggie whispered.

I shook my head. "I don't... I'm not sure." That was mostly because I was afraid of what we might find inside. What if the killer had murdered more than just Allen? What if he or she had killed someone else and had dumped the body in the trunk? I took an involuntary step back.

But then common sense kicked in. It had been a week since Victor said Allen had died. Assuming that if whoever killed him had killed another at the same time, then a body in the trunk of the car in the heat would be smelling by now. Badly. And there would most certainly be flies buzzing about the trunk, trying to get in.

The car was an older model; not as old as mine, but it wasn't one of the newer, computerized jobs like Maggie had. "I wonder..." I tried the passenger door handle, not surprised to find it was unlocked. From the looks of the car, Allen probably wouldn't have cared if raccoons nested inside. Maybe they already have...

My nose crinkled from the stale odor in the car, most likely from the food containers. I reached in and opened the glove box, then smiled when I saw the button inside and pushed it.

"Hey, the trunk just opened!" Maggie cried. I looked over to where she'd been standing a few feet from the back of the car.

She was backing up, a horrified look on her face. I hurried over to her, turning to look at the trunk while trying to brace myself for what I might see.

But I didn't see anything.

"What's the matter?" I asked Maggie in a hushed voice. "What did you see?"

She shook her head. "Nothing, but…" She slowly turned her bulging eyes toward me. "It opened by itself," she whispered. "I think the car is haunted."

I huffed. "I opened it, you ninny!" I snapped as I stomped over to the trunk, forgetting that I might discover something awful.

I did.

Inside the trunk was a lot more junk, Trash, really. I was starting to think Allen was a hoarder and had the unkind thought that maybe it was better he'd died so soon after renting the cabin, or else Todd likely would have had a mess on his hands once Allen left.

With a wince, I glanced heavenward. *Sorry Lord… that was mean.*

Turning my attention back to the trunk, I examined it more closely. On top of the pile of empty plastic shopping bags was another line of dried blood. There was a pair of jeans that also had what looked like blood.

My hand went to my mouth—and right back down again as I gagged when realizing I might have inadvertently touched… dead things in my examination.

"Did you just spit?"

I jumped, hitting my head on the trunk lid before turning to glare at Maggie as I rubbed yet a second head lump caused by her in the past ten minutes.

She crossed her arms. "Madelyn May Kaye, I declare, that was just rude!" Maggie sniffed. "Ladies shouldn't spit."

"Don't sneak up on me like that!" I hissed, ignoring her

comment. Yes, I had spit, but it was only because I thought I might have something gross in my mouth... but I wasn't going to bother explaining myself.

I continued rubbing the bump as I looked in the trunk once more. But I couldn't spot any more evidence unless I moved some things around, which I most certainly did not want to do.

"Remind me to bring gloves and maybe a mask the next time we do something like this." I swatted away a little fly then, wondering if it was going to head into the car since I'd left the door open. With all the food containers in there, he'd have plenty to eat.

Yuck.

I stepped back as I thought. The little car really did look like it had been abandoned in the woods. When I'd first seen it amongst the trees, I thought it looked like someone had been trying to hide it. But now... it reminded me of the cars one would see in a junky backyard. Unusable and forgotten.

In fact, the more I looked at it, the more it looked like it was unusable. I turned toward the cabin to consider the meadow versus the location of the car. Allen would have had to come up the drive, pull along the front of the cabin and then basically drive right into the midst of the trees.

On closer examination, I could see where the trees had scraped the sides of the car as it passed through. I stepped around to the driver's side, noting deep gouges in the paint. The front fender was bent as well, though I frowned when I realized it was bent out, not in, as if it had caught on something while backing.

"I wonder if the car popped out of gear and rolled here," I wondered out loud. Maggie was right behind me, so she of course thought I was talking to her.

"It's an automatic," she said, surprising me with her astuteness. I peered in the driver's window and saw that she was right.

Well, that killed the gear popping idea. But it was also odd that the car's gearshift was in the Park position, which meant that the car had been driven through the trees, hit the tree stump, and then put in park.

My frown increased as I pushed through the undergrowth to get to the front of the car.

"Watch for ticks!" Maggie called.

"Not helpful," I told her as I stepped down on a dead bush, mashing it into the ground. "How do you 'look for ticks'?" I asked. "They're basically invisible until they embed themselves in your leg." Another involuntary shudder ran through me at the thought. I hated all blood-sucking creatures.

Once I got enough brush pushed away, I took a closer look at the car. The entire front end was dented in, to the point I doubted it would be drivable. The grill was shattered where it had hit the stump, and the plastic part that was normally attached under the bumper was on the ground. Why Allen had plowed his car into the trees was a big mystery and I considered all the possibilities.

Maybe he'd been drunk. Or possibly he'd been ill, so sick that he didn't know what he was doing. There was also the idea that he might have been injured, or perhaps poisoned...

"Now I'm starting to sound like one of his novels," I laughed to myself.

"You mean like this?" Maggie called and I looked up to see she'd opened the driver's side back door and was holding one of Allen's books. She thumbed through it.

"Yeah, like that," I mumbled as I rubbed my chin with my finger while I stared at the car. There was just something not right about it, about the damage, but I was having a dickens of a time figuring it out.

I thought about calling Robert and asking him for a recommendation for an autobody repair person to get an opinion, but that would lead to questions that I most certainly didn't want to answer. The man would not be happy that Maggie and I were doing our own investigation, and he'd probably rat us out to Jonny... not that the incompetent boob would care.

Sighing, I started to walk back around to the passenger side when something caught my eye. I squinted and moved closer to the car, letting loose with a little shriek when I smacked into a branch that caught my hair.

"What's wrong?" Maggie called. "Did you get a tick? I told you to watch out for them!"

"No, I did not get a tick," I growled as I yanked my hair off the branch, wincing when a good chunk of it caught. I rubbed yet another sore spot on my scalp as I leaned over and examined the passenger side of the bumper.

Like the rest of the front end, it was destroyed. But that was what had caught my eye… the bumper on the driver's side was bent out at an angle, which was understandable since the thing had been pushed in right in the middle where it had creamed the stump. But the passenger side wasn't popped out. I supposed that wouldn't be unusual in and of itself, but what was unusual was the fact that not only was it not popped out, it was dented in.

And on the cracked plastic bumper, there was another spot of dried blood.

"Maggie, don't touch anything," I told her as I backed away from the car, running into a tree. I cursed myself for my clumsiness; if I didn't quit hitting my head I was going to look like a bumpy toad.

"What? Why?" she asked as she glanced up from the book she still held.

"We need to wipe our fingerprints off the car," I said by way of answer. "What else did you touch in there?" I pointed at the backseat.

"Nothing," she said with a dramatic shudder. "It's disgusting in there. I just picked up the book."

"Well, take it with you," I said as I pushed back out of the brush to the driver's side. I contemplated if we should in fact wipe our fingerprints from the door handles, or if that would destroy other fingerprints that might be there. While I didn't want to get questioned by the police department boobs, I also

103

didn't want to take the chance of ruining the evidence.

I decided we'd just have to come up with some excuse for why we were here, why we were checking out the car if it came up. But then I thought about the fact that our fingerprints shouldn't be on file anywhere; it wasn't like either of us had ever been arrested. Still...

"But I haven't paid for it," Maggie protested, drawing me out of my thoughts. I gave her a look.

"I don't think Allen will mind," I drawled. Her cheeks colored and she nodded shakily, rather like one of those dogs with the bouncing heads that you put in your back car window.

The thought drew my gaze to the car's back dash, fully expecting to see a Taco Bell Chihuahua there, but it was clear, except for what looked like a shirt. The open trunk drew my eyes, though, and I moved around to the back.

"We need to close this without touching it."

Maggie came to stand beside me. "Why don't you just close it the same way you opened it?" She turned toward me. "How did you do that anyway?"

I sighed; I would have to wipe my fingerprints from the glovebox and the trunk button at least. There really wasn't any way I could explain why I'd gotten in there.

"There's a button in the car, but it only opens it."

She took a step toward the car. "Well, then we'll have to close it the old-fashioned—"

I shrieked just as she reached up. "Don't touch it!" I scolded her. "We have to make sure we don't get our fingerprints all over it. Might mess up the investigation." That was assuming Jonny actually did his job for once.

Maggie nodded. "Good thinking," she said as she started unbuttoning her blouse. I frowned at her in horror.

"What are you doing?" I shrieked again. "You can't be that hot!"

She rolled her eyes at me. "I'm going to use my blouse to

close the trunk," she said haughtily, like I was the brain-cell challenged one of the two of us.

"Fine," I griped as I glanced around. It wasn't like anyone was going to see her in her bra. Of course, she'd probably have no problem with it.

Maggie pulled her blouse off, then wrapped it around her hands before reaching up to yank the trunk lid down.

"Just grab the edge!" I warned. "Don't want to accidentally wipe it."

She nodded and did as I instructed, but once it was down, it didn't latch. "Great," I mumbled as I put my hand out. "Give me your blouse."

Maggie held it to her chest. "It won't fit you," she protested.

I tilted my chin down and stared at her over my glasses. "One, we're the same size, ding dong. And two, I just want to use it to push the trunk down!"

The corners of her mouth turned down—likely at the reminder we both were hefty women—but she handed me the blouse. I wadded it up and then pushed on the top of the lid until it clicked.

"There," I said as we both stepped back. I handed the blouse back to her and she started griping when she saw the dust all over it. "Just shake it out," I muttered, though I was distracted. Because, right on the back of the trunk were two very distinct handprints.

Someone had pushed the car into the trees.

Chapter 11

"DON'T YOU GET snippy with me, young man!" The growl I gave Jonny after my comment was most certainly unladylike—not that I cared—but it served its purpose when his eyes widened, and he took a step back.

"You're the one who wanted to write off the death as an accident," I went on, keeping my finger pointed at his chest. I was starting to be very sorry we hadn't made an anonymous call to the Crown Hill Police like Maggie had suggested, but I knew they would have figured out it was us anyway.

Jonny's face reddened in anger as he swung his hand out toward Allen's car. "You shouldn't have been here investigating—"

"Someone needed to!" I interrupted the buffoon. "The good Lord knows you weren't—going to." I barely stopped myself from saying "you weren't capable of doing it," and mentally patted myself on the back for being discerning. That comment likely wouldn't have gone over too well with the banty rooster.

He had the nerve to take a step toward me. I hate to admit that I was a little bit intimidated, but I certainly didn't let it show as I crossed my arms over my chest and glared at him.

His finger pointed at my face, much like I had done to him. "I'm tired of telling you to quit trying to do my job," he yelled.

"There isn't any reason to be upset," Maggie butted in. I'm sure she thought she was going to soothe the situation, but Jonny just looked angrier at having two women standing against him.

"Now, we could stand here and argue until the cows turn blue," she went on; I had to bite the inside of my cheek to keep from correcting her, "but that isn't going to get the crime solved, is it?" she asked reasonably.

Jonny had a confused look that quickly faded into another scowl. "I don't need advice from a deranged cuckoo bird," he spat.

I sucked in a breath; the idiot should have learned his lesson that I didn't take kindly to others insulting Maggie. That was my job.

"Now look, you—"

"Maddie!" I turned my scowl toward Robert, who was walking across the meadow toward where we stood near Allen's car. The man had interrupted my tirade and his sunny smile took the wind out of my snippy ship's sails.

"How are you, honey?" he asked as he walked up and surprised me by sliding an arm around my waist as he kissed my cheek. "Don't peck at the little bug," he whispered in my ear, "he's not worth getting gravel in your beak."

While wondering if that comment was due to Jonny's calling Maggie a cuckoo, I gave Robert the hairy eyeball as he stepped away, which just made his grin widen. *This man*, I laughed to myself. Robert seemed to be the only one capable of smoothing my frayed edges.

"I didn't even hear you pull up," I said by way of greeting.

"That's because your hearing is bad," Maggie chimed in. The look I shot her way made her smile fade. Why she was smiling was anyone's guess; apparently, she didn't realize Jonny had just insulted her. Knowing Maggie, she probably thought the comment had been directed at me.

"Grandpap, why are you here?" Jonny asked with a whine. Robert looked at the kid, eyebrow raised.

"Because my woman is here," he said pleasantly. While I knew Robert was just saying that to pull his grandson's chain, the words still warmed me.

The words had the intended effect; Jonny's mouth turned down and he spun around and stalked off. He immediately started giving orders to Rick Largo, the lowest man on the police totem pole, who obviously was tasked with fingerprinting, judging by the mess he was making of the already dirty car.

I was still a little worried about our fingerprints being found and traced to us, though it was unlikely. Maggie and I had discussed it before the police arrived and the plan was to play dumb.

I knew Maggie was up to the task.

"So... want to tell me what's going on?" Robert asked. I glanced up at him and sighed. He wasn't going to like the fact that Maggie and I were out doing our own investigation.

"No."

That made him laugh. Before I could say anything else, Maggie added her pearls.

"We found Allen's car in the trees and the thing is a mess! Why, I can't imagine the poor man kept his car in such a state. I'm just certain it was a boggart that did it. Mischievous creatures," she said with a head shake.

I glanced at Robert, who shrugged. *No idea*, he mouthed.

Maggie crossed her arms and tapped her chin with her forefinger before shaking it. "Of course, it could also be limoneads," she said as she glanced around the area. "They *are* protective of their meadows. Maybe they didn't like having the car there and they trashed it."

"What in the world are you talking about?" I snapped. I swore the woman was one sandwich shy of a picnic.

Maggie blinked a few times, as if just realizing she was talking out loud. "Oh," she giggled, "I was talking about mythological creatures. You know, since we have a dragon on the loose and all, I figured we probably have more of the things out and about."

"Oh, for Pete's—"

"Maggie," Robert said gently, interrupting my oncoming tirade, "we talked about the fact that Al... er, that the body wasn't burned by a dragon."

I glared at him, though he wasn't looking at me. Sometimes, the man was a real fun sucker, ruining my rant and all.

"It was an accident, remember?" he added.

The woman nodded, though she winked at me. Conspiratorially, like I agreed with her lunacy. I rolled my eyes at her.

"Anyway," I drawled as I gave Maggie a look before turning my attention back to Robert, "there's no way I'm going to convince you we're not out here doing our own investigation, so, shocking revelation—that's what we're doing."

Robert chuckled at my admission. "Yeah, I figured," he said with a crooked grin, then glanced toward the car before leaning in close.

"And what did you find that you're not going to share with Jonny?"

That made my own grin appear and I turned to walk toward the cabin. There was no way I wanted that banty police detective overhearing what I'd discovered. He needed to learn to do his own investigating. Once we were completely out of earshot, I looked at Robert.

I waved between Maggie and myself. "We noticed the car looked a little strange between the trees, so we went over to investigate it."

"After we went in the cabin," Maggie added. I whipped my head toward her and widened my eyes. I hadn't planned on telling Robert we were guilty of breaking and entering.

"Oh, you did, did you?" he asked, though he was staring at me.

"Used the key Todd left," I shrugged, hoping the man would think Todd had no problem with us being there. "But we didn't find anything," I lied. I could swear the ring in my pocket was heating up.

Liar, liar, pants on fire had a new meaning. If Maggie were in my shoes—or, rather, in my pants—she'd be swearing that the ring was the cause of Allen's combustion.

"Anyway," I hurried on, trying to deflect Robert from prying while I silently asked God to forgive me for the sort of lie, "when we checked out the car, Maggie noticed blood near the trunk. I went around the thing and saw the front bumper had been caved in." I waved toward the car.

"There were handprints on the back, so it was kind of obvious it had been pushed there," I continued. "And the front bumper is smashed in where it hit a tree stump. But I don't think that's all the car hit."

Robert's eyebrows rose at that. "What do you mean?"

"The front passenger side was smashed in, separate from the tree stump," I explained. "And there was some blood."

He considered that. "Deer?"

I shook my head, but Maggie said, "Yes?" We both turned to her in confusion. She looked confused herself.

Her shoulders lifted a little. "I thought Robert was trying to get my attention."

I frowned for a moment, before I realized what she meant. "He meant *deer* as in venison, not *dear* as in sweetheart. And besides, do you really think Robert would call you 'dear'?"

She shrugged again. "Well, maybe. The other day he called me 'sugar'."

I lifted a brow and looked at the man. "What?" he sputtered. "I did not!"

Maggie was nodding before he could finish the denial. "Yes, you did, remember? At the bakery when we were having coffee, I asked you to pass the creamer and when you handed it to me you called me 'sugar'," she said a bit dreamily. I kind of wanted to punch her.

Robert laughed. "I was asking if you wanted the sugar along with the creamer."

Maggie's face heated once again, but I ignored it as I looked back at Robert. "Maybe a deer," I allowed. "Something tall enough to be smacked by the bumper."

He nodded slightly as he looked over at the officers looking in the car. His face suddenly morphed into a thunderous expression, and he stomped away without a word.

"For the love of Pete," he shouted as he crossed the meadow, "you can't just rifle through the trunk like that! There might be evidence in there you're destroying!"

We watched him dress down Rick, who hung his head like a puppy who'd gotten caught piddling on the carpet, then Robert walked over to Jonny. He pulled him to the front of the car and pointed at the bumper.

"Come on," I told Maggie, "let's go get a sandwich." I'd text Robert and tell him where we were heading so he could join us if he wanted to.

"Kirby's?" she asked happily as we headed toward her car. I nearly groaned when I saw she'd put Allen's book that she'd taken from his car on her dashboard where God and all creation could see it. Thankfully, the Crown Hill nincompoop PD hadn't noticed it.

"Yeah, that's fine," I sighed. It would be the third time that week we'd eaten at Kirby's, and while I loved their food, the same thing all the time got a little old. Plus, there was that combustion problem with Maggie. Her crabcake farts made even Wally whine. Cat poop was the dog's favorite delicacy, so that was saying a lot.

As usual during tourist season, Kirby's was packed. We had to wait for a table but were blessed when a couple decided to take theirs to go when their young one started acting up.

We hadn't even ordered when Maggie waved at someone who walked in. I had my back to the door and assumed it was Robert, though the man hadn't answered my text invitation.

"Come sit with us," she called, which was, of course, my alert that it wasn't Robert. I turned in my chair and my jaw nearly dropped when I saw Edwin Evans walking toward us, his usual scowl on his face.

"I'll sit with you if you don't ask me a bunch of ridiculous questions about my books," he said with a pointed glare in my direction when he reached the table. I offered what was likely a fanatical smile in return.

"Oh, she won't ask you any questions," Maggie said with a

111

wave of her hand. "Once she starts eating, nothing comes out of that mouth. Well, except crumbs."

While I glared at her for the disparaging remark in front of my author idol, Edwin actually chuckled while he lowered himself into the chair. I think my mouth dropped open again; I didn't think the brusque man even knew how to smile, much less laugh.

Maggie had the nerve to instruct the man on what to order, and how to order it. "You have to get the crabcake sandwich with extra sauce," she told him. "And the curly fries go best with it. Or onion rings."

"Maybe I'll get both," Edwin told her with a wink.

For the third time in ten minutes, my jaw dropped. *The* Edwin Evans was flirting with Maggie? What universe did I accidentally teleport into? And to make matters even stranger, Maggie—who never met a male she didn't like—wasn't flirting back.

Naomi walked up to take our order and pointed her pen at Edwin. "Sorry sir, this is a no-smoking place."

My eyes traveled to Edwin's hand. Sure enough, he was holding a cigar. I hadn't even noticed it, not with all the weirdness going on around the table. He held it up.

"Ain't lit," he told Naomi. "Had to quit smoking nearly a year ago. Just like to carry the things around and pretend." He actually gave the middle-aged woman a smile, though it wasn't flirtatious. Apparently, it was just me he didn't like, I thought with a sigh.

We placed our orders and Maggie chatted about places Edwin should visit while he was staying in Crown Hill. I just sat and listened, grateful when Naomi returned with our drinks right away. My throat had gotten really parched, what with all the hard swallowing I'd been doing since Edwin joined us.

Several moments went by when Edwin looked at me. "What's the matter with you?" he said, all niceness gone. I didn't understand how he could be so pleasant with Maggie and even Naomi, but whenever he looked at me, it was with a scowl.

"Nothing's the matter," I muttered as I took another swallow of my tea. I noticed that Edwin liked his as syrupy sweet as Maggie did. Between the two of them, they'd created a mountain of empty sugar packets.

"Seems the cat's got your tongue," he continued.

A small grin lifted my lips, but Maggie made a distressed noise and we both looked at her. I waited for something stupid to come out of her mouth, likely asking which cat had stolen my tongue, but she surprised me.

"I forgot to tell you," she said as she turned to me, "Bixby keeps trying to escape. Twice this week, I've found the screen on the cat's window pushed out."

I frowned. "Well, close the window," I told her reasonably. "We don't know if that cat has all her shots, or even if she's fixed. We don't need her out roaming until we get that taken care of."

Maggie shook her head. "The girls don't go outside; you know that. But I keep the window open for fresh air for them. Bixby is just going to have to learn the rules." She turned to Edwin.

"Bixby is… um, was, Allen's cat. I was pet-sitting for him so he could get his book done, but, well, you know."

I watched Edwin closely to look for any guilt. His expression didn't change much, though; his crinkled face still looked a bit like a bulldog. He nodded.

"That was mighty nice of you," he told Maggie, who smiled in return. Again, in a non-flirtatious way. She was acting so strange, I almost felt compelled to check her for a temperature.

"Though I doubted it did much good," he went on. "That man was so far behind on his second book that Denlaw—our mutual publisher—was threatening to sue for breach of contract." Edwin shook his head.

"He had a deadline back in March that he missed, and they gave him ninety days to provide seventy-five percent of the manuscript. Doubt he made that deadline either."

After reading the awful bit of writing Allen had on his laptop, I didn't think that was such a bad thing. Before I could speak, Naomi brought our food, and we all thanked her and waited until she walked away. Maggie and I grasped our hands and I was a bit surprised when she grabbed Edwin's with the other.

"We always say grace before meals," she declared. The man shocked me by smiling and reaching across the table to take my hand so we could complete the circle.

"Do you mind if I do the honors?" Edwin asked. I almost fell out of my chair. We both nodded, and I could tell Maggie was nearly as surprised as I was.

"Father God, we thank You for the food. Thank You for all the other blessings in our lives. Keep us safe and in Your loving care today and always. Amen."

I barely squeaked out my "amen" when Edwin tightened his grip on my hand just slightly, like a mini hug. I had never understood the term "fangirl" until that moment. My favorite author was not only eating lunch with me, but he'd also held my hand and even prayed...

The day was going to be marked on my calendar.

"Looks like I'm a little too late." I looked up with a smile when I heard Robert's voice. He took the empty chair next to mine and reached out to shake Edwin's hand. Before I could introduce the two men, Naomi was already heading our way. She adored Robert, as did most of Crown Hill.

"Hey, Chief, what'll ya have?"

He gave the waitress a friendly smile. "Usual," he said with a glance at me. "Except make it a diet soda," he whined, before sighing dramatically. I gave him a long-suffering look, then glanced at Edwin.

"Robert is prediabetic," I explained. "Edwin Evans, this is my, uh..." I paused, reminding myself to figure out how I should introduce the man. "This is Robert Donovan. He was police chief here for many years and everyone seems to think he still is."

Edwin nodded at Robert. "We already met," he said around a few curly fries.

Robert nodded as he reached out to take the drink from Naomi. He took a small sip, then winced. I laughed, because I knew how much he hated diet soda.

"Robert came to the cabin after y'all found Roger's body," Edwin continued. Maggie made a strange noise and we all looked at her.

"You said 'y'all'," she told the man. He smiled fully for the first time, and I realized then he really wasn't that bad looking at all. Much less bulldoggish than I thought.

"Guess my Texas is showin'," he said with an exaggerated drawl.

"I thought you were from New York!" I blurted.

Edwin glanced my way. "Just lived in Albany for the past thirty years or so. Most of the south has been worked out of me, but it slips out sometimes."

"Oh, a southern man," Maggie breathed, showing more interest in Edwin. Before she started going on about how wonderful southerners were, I spoke again.

"So, about that breach of contract—" I glanced at Robert who had a questioning look. I shook my head slightly, knowing he'd understand that I'd fill him in later.

"What would have happened if Allen missed the second deadline?"

Edwin shrugged, then washed his mouthful down with his tea, which I appreciated. "If his contract was the same as mine usually are, then he would have had to pay back his advance. Probably be sued for damages, too, if Denlaw had done much advertising for the sequel. But I doubt they had, considering Rogers' first book crashed and burned." He paused and tilted his head. "Though I did hear he'd had a sudden surge in paperback sales just before he left to come here."

Which might explain all those boxes of books in the car... But that made no sense; why would Allen buy his own books?

Was he trying to ensure he got on some bestselling list? Or maybe he'd been planning on selling the books himself. Maybe he was just trying to make himself look good to Denlaw Publishing.

But Edwin made that sound like a lost cause.

Chapter 12

ALL THE WAY home Maggie was quiet, which was strange for her, especially after spending any time with an available man. Usually, she went on and on about how funny they were, how handsome, sexy, drool-worthy, whatever she thought they were and by the time we'd get home, I'd fully expected her to start writing "Mrs. Maggie Whatever His Name Was" in a notebook like some preteen.

But even though she and Edwin had seemed to have quite a bit in common—other than just being from the southern side of the USA—she didn't seem interested in the guy. Frankly, it was odd.

"You and Edwin sure seemed to like the same things," I said when we were stopped at a light. Maggie was so distracted that she'd actually been obeying all the traffic laws.

I was starting to worry about her.

"Hmm?" she murmured as she glanced at me. "Oh... yeah." She shrugged. "He and I grew up much the same."

"Hillbilly?" I teased. Usually when I called her a hillbilly, she'd get very upset, but again, just a lift of the shoulders.

"We're about the same age as Edwin, don't you think?" I already knew Edwin was a year older than us, but I was just trying to make conversation.

The light changed, but Maggie turned to stare at me in horror. The car behind honked, so she shook her head and took off.

"No, we're not the same age!" she protested. "He's much older," she declared with a shoulder shake as she straightened in her seat, looking most put-out.

I gave her a look that she didn't catch, since she was thankfully watching the road for once. "Actually, he's only a year older than us."

That drew her attention to me for longer than a split second. I motioned out the windshield, a hint that she needed to watch where she was going. Her lips pursed, but she turned back to her driving.

"Why did you ask me if you already knew the answer?" she griped.

I didn't bother answering but pointed to the cross street ahead. "Let's stop by and see if Victor found anything out about... you know."

Maggie glanced at me. "You don't have to keep kitty toeing around me. I'm not a child. We can say Allen's name, you know."

"It's 'pussy footing'," I said by way of response.

She turned her upper body toward me with a shocked look. "Madelyn May! Your language!"

"Watch where you're going!" I yelled when she swerved onto the shoulder and almost took out a speed limit sign. Maggie jerked the wheel back just in time.

"And I didn't say anything wrong," I grumbled. We didn't speak again until she parked at the funeral home. There were five other cars in the lot, which was a bit disheartening. Since the only employees at the funeral home were Victor and Molly Pedersen, I figured they had some customers.

"Well," I said as I opened my door, "I guess Victor is going to be too busy to talk to us, but we can at least make a payment on our plan." I hated the idea of planning my own funeral—not to mention the irksome expense—but it was better to be prepared than leave it up to your loved ones. That had been a hard lesson to learn after Frank's passing.

Maggie followed, though she pointed at one of the cars. "Isn't that Bill Crane's car?" I looked where she pointed and nodded.

"Yeah, and that's Missy's car next to it. Wonder if Granny finally died." Missus Crane was one of Crown Hill's oldest citizens, though no one knew exactly how old she was.

Speculation was she'd been around during the biblical flood. All her children had already passed and only two grandkids remained, plus a handful of greats, but the old gal lingered on. Everyone said Granny had died ages ago but was too stubborn to admit it.

"I just saw her driving down Pelican the other day!" Maggie exclaimed. "She couldn't be dead."

I paused and turned to her, eyebrow raised. "Why not? She could have died anytime between then and now."

Maggie shook her head. "You don't just die. There's a process you have to go through."

My whole face scrunched up at that, so hard my glasses went askew. I fixed them as I exclaimed incredulously, "What?" but then I waved my hand. "No, never mind," I said just as Maggie opened her mouth to explain whatever stupid thing she'd come up with.

"I don't want to know. Let's just see if we can get a minute to talk to Victor under the pretense of paying our bill." Maggie was still pouting when we walked inside the lobby.

Thankfully, Molly was tied up with Bill and Missy, along with someone else I didn't recognize from the back. Molly waved at us through the office door.

"We're just going to talk to Victor," I told her as we moved to that hidden door. Molly just nodded as she continued talking to the family.

"Sorry I'm late!" came a yell just as the front door opened. "Blasted construction down on Peacock. Had to cut across the dairy's back field to avoid it. Just 'bout took out a cow, but managed to miss it. Too bad—mighta gotten some steak out of it."

Maggie and I turned to see Granny—aka, Mabel Smithson—hobble into the lobby. She nodded at us, then headed to the office.

"You get the kid's casket picked out yet?" she hollered as she walked in.

I glanced at Maggie. "Starting to think that old crow is never going to fly the coop."

Maggie looked at me with wide eyes. "I think she's a vampire," she whispered. "You know—immortal."

My eyeballs hurt from the restraint of not rolling them.

Victor was in the examination room. I hated to go in there, but if we wanted to talk to the man, it was a necessity. I cringed when I saw three bodies on the exam tables... covered, thankfully.

He glanced up from a table where he'd been writing in a notebook. I was a bit surprised to see him wearing reading glasses. They made the strange man appear more human and less Saturday night horror movie host.

"Ladies," he said by way of greeting, then glanced at the bodies, probably to make sure they weren't uncovered, "what can I do for you?" He took his glasses off and set them on the notebook. It made me wonder if he even used a computer.

"Well, we came by to make a payment on our funeral plans, but Molly was busy. Guess another of Granny's kids died?"

Victor glanced at the table next to him. Whoever was underneath the white cover had a very rotund belly. It reminded me of a snow-covered dome like you'd see on a ski slope.

"Grandchild, actually. Umberto."

I nodded, while Maggie made a tsking sound. "He was such a handsome young man," she gushed. "How did he die?"

"Sudden cardiac arrest," Victor said absently.

"But he was so young!" Maggie protested. Victor and I exchanged a glance.

"He was sixty-four," Victor said. "Not that young." He winced when he realized who he was talking to. "I mean, for having a heart attack," he rushed on. "And Umberto was a smoker and had diabetes. High blood pressure too."

Maggie put a hand to her chest, and I once again refrained

120

from rolling my eyes, but just barely. The woman was a borderline hypochondriac and would probably announce she was having chest pains at any moment.

I wonder what she would have done if Victor had said Umberto had died of prostate cancer.

Shaking those thoughts, I decided to be point-blank with the coroner. "And what did you find out about Allen Rogers?"

Victor glanced toward the tables again and I wondered if Allen's body was in there too. Though it was cold in the examination room, I didn't think it was cold enough to preserve a body, the thought of which made my lip curl before I could stop it.

"I shouldn't tell you…"

"Oh, for the love of—you keep saying that, but you keep giving us the info anyway, so just tell us!" I snapped. Victor's long face colored for a moment, which honestly was a much better look on the guy. Better than his usual pasty, cemetery haunting ghoul face anyway.

Be nice, Maddie, I scolded myself.

Victor sighed, but he nodded. "Well, since you were the ones who alerted me to the fact that there might be a crime, I guess you're entitled. But it is now a criminal investigation, so don't go sharing the information," he warned. We both nodded.

"My lips are zipped and I'm throwing away the key," Maggie said. Both Victor and I stared at her for a moment, then he shook his head slightly and pointedly looked at me.

"The body had been injured," he started.

"Well, yeah, he was burned," Maggie said. I pinched her arm.

"Ow!"

"Go on," I encouraged Victor while Maggie rubbed her arm and glared at me, which I ignored.

The man's lips twitched, I'm sure due to our antics. "As I mentioned before, I had suspicions the victim had been in an accident—"

"Yes, he was—" Maggie started to interrupt again, then squealed when I tried to pinch her. She managed to get away just before I got her on the side that time.

Victor couldn't stop the chuckle that time. Shaking his head, he continued. "The x-rays showed several fractures—legs, one arm, ribs. I'm sure there were more, but with the condition of the body, that was all I could determine."

I stared at the coroner for a moment, wondering if I could trust him like he was trusting us. I finally decided I was going to have to. "I don't want to give the police any help," I said, "so this is between you and me—"

"And me!" Maggie added. I gave her a look that caused her to inch away, completely out of pinching range.

"Between us," I relented with a sigh, "but Allen's car had been in an accident. Hit something big, from the looks of it." Both Victor and I looked toward the bodies. I assumed the last one at the far end was Allen's, which made me wonder who was in the middle. Our town was small enough that I knew most people, outside of summertime.

"Hmm," Victor said as he put a gloved hand to his chin. It made me grimace, wondering what all might be on that glove.

"That would be consistent with the injuries, if he was hit from the front." He seemed to be talking to himself, so I just let him ramble on about the injuries, a lot of medical jargon I didn't understand.

"But if it was Allen's car, how could he have hit himself?"

I turned to look at Maggie and she flinched. "That's a good question," I said. Her relief was almost laughable. I glanced back at Victor.

"Well, I guess the investigation is still on the table, so we'll probably be seeing you around."

The smile he gave us looked pretty forced.

WE WENT TO the grocery store and then headed home to spend some time with Wally and "the girls." And I still needed to talk to Elle, to see if she'd fill me in on what was going on with her. It was doubtful; the woman was still holding a bit of a grudge with me, but it was getting a little better.

"You know what would be nice?" Maggie asked as she unloaded the bag she carried. Though the house had been split into two separate living quarters, we shared the living room and kitchen—along with the groceries.

"What?" I had to fight back a curse—which for me would have been something like "darn"—when I saw that Maggie had moved all the cans of cat food into the cabinet with the canned goods of human food.

"It would be nice if we could take the pets with us to the bakery," she said from inside the refrigerator. I had to ask her to repeat it, since I couldn't be sure that's what she'd said.

I nodded. "Yeah, it would, but I'm pretty sure it's not legal." There were so many health regulations we had to follow just to serve danishes, I seriously doubted we could get by with dogs and cats inside.

"Maybe we could rent the place next door. The Murphys are closing the bookstore and moving to Maryland next month. Maybe we could turn it into some sort of pet cafe."

Pretty sure my jaw unhinged. "That's actually a fantastic idea! Why, I think there are so many people who would love to have their animals join them. We could sell the food in the bakery and have them take it next door with their pets. It's the perfect solution!"

Maggie preened under the praise. "I think so too. I really miss the girls. I thought it would be enough to cut back on our hours at the bakery and have more time at home, but it's not. We spend so much time running around doing other things."

I nodded. That was certainly true. Just that day we'd been

all over the place and hadn't spent any time at all with the pets.

"It would be nice to have them nearby," I agreed. "But you've got to think about the fact most people don't take their cats out with them. It's going to be almost all dogs. And you know how dogs can be with cats."

Maggie closed the refrigerator and turned around, looking confused. "How are they?"

I gave her another look that I'm sure she didn't interpret correctly. "Dogs and cats..." I waited for the lightbulb to click on, but it didn't.

"They're sworn enemies!" I huffed. Honestly, it was amazing how the woman had lived to be as old as she had. With as dopey as she was, I was surprised she hadn't done something like drown in the shower by now.

"But Wally gets along with the girls," Maggie said, her brows creasing in the middle.

I pulled my glasses off and rubbed my eyes. "Remember when Wally brought the baby raccoon home in his mouth... and it was completely unharmed?" She nodded.

Putting my glasses back on, I propped my hand on my hip as I sighed. I really wanted to go talk to Elle and then park my hiney on the sofa for a few hours. "And there was the time the ducks followed him in the house. Remember that?" Another nod.

"Wally isn't your average dog. Besides being a Golden Retriever, a breed known for being overly sweet and affectionate, he's also a lover boy. All creatures great and small are his buddies. But you can't judge all dogs by his behavior. Wally is one of a kind."

Maggie shrugged. "I suppose. I've always been a cat person. Wally is the only dog I've been around."

She'd said that before, but I never believed her. At least, I thought she'd been exaggerating. But after that comment, I wondered if it was true. And I also wondered how it was possible to go through seventy-plus years and not be around a dog.

Sometimes I thought Maggie had been hatched just before I met her ten years prior.

I managed to keep my thoughts to myself. "We might be able to separate the bakery and the Murphy's place, kind of like we did with the house. I'll call Todd tomorrow and have him come over to talk about it."

Maggie grinned. "Jasmin will be happy."

I gave her a look, but she wasn't wrong. My granddaughter had a big crush on Todd and I had a feeling it was reciprocated. Though I thought the man was too old for her and I was hoping she'd set her cap on James, there wasn't anything I could do to stop a relationship with Todd from happening. Jasmin was an adult, which she constantly reminded me.

The bedroom door was closed, so I knocked softly. Elle and Jasmin were supposed to run the bakery the afternoons Maggie and I took off, but Elle had been too tired—or sick—to help out. Thankfully, Jasmin was very capable on her own and James was more than happy to help her out whenever he didn't have deliveries.

Elle's voice was too muffled to make out, so I opened the door a crack. "Hey hon, it's Mom. How are you feeling?"

The covers rustled as Elle tried to sit up. My eyes widened when I realized she seemed like she just didn't have the strength to do so. I pushed the door open and hurried to her side.

Pulling the pillows up, I helped her rearrange herself until she was propped upright. Wally decided to make an appearance then and jumped up on the bed. I started to shoo him, but Elle stopped me.

She sunk her fingers into the thick fur at his neck. "I always loved dogs," she smiled. I smiled with her, remembering how we'd always had a dog when she was growing up.

Elle stared at Wally and baby-talked to him, which the big guy ate up. He rolled over on his back for a tummy rub while I examined Elle. I didn't like what I saw.

My daughter was even thinner than she'd been when she and Jasmin had first shown up. The skin clung to her cheekbones and sagged under her arms, which jiggled as she rubbed Wally. Dark circles surrounded her eyes that were a bit sunken. She looked far older than her forty years.

Elle also looked sick. Very sick.

"Honey," I murmured as I sat on the other side of her. I waited until Elle looked at me in question and I smiled softly. "What's wrong?" I'd thought she might be depressed over the situation with Carl and all, but after not seeing her for a handful of days, the shock of her appearance led me to believe it was far worse than that.

"Nothing's wrong, Mom," Elle said. "I'm just tired."

I shook my head. "I hope you don't think I'm that stupid," I said sternly. "Now, either you truly don't know what's wrong with you, or else you do and you're not sharing. Which is it?"

Elle's frail shoulders lifted, then dropped. It was as if more life drained from her in that moment, which was a terrifying thought. But her next words were even more horrific.

"I'm dying of cancer."

Chapter 13

"I WANT HIM charged!" I yelled when Robert opened his door. I'd been so angry after Elle and I had talked before she got so exhausted she fell asleep right in the middle of a sentence that I'd taken Wally and driven to Robert's house.

The man blinked a few times as he opened the door wider to let me in. Wally didn't hesitate as he barreled right past us and made himself at home on Robert's recliner.

"Okay," he said slowly when I brushed past. I doubted Robert had ever seen me really truly angry. I was probably scaring the man, but at the moment I couldn't find it in me to care.

"Mind telling me who?" he asked as he sank to the sofa. I was too keyed up to sit, so I paced in front of him. Both Robert and Wally watched me with wary eyes. The poor dog had already listened to me rant all the way over.

"Carl," I said, snarling over the jerk's name. "Elle's husband, Jazz's dad. I want him charged with... with... arg!" I threw my hands in the air in frustration, unsure of what the crime would be.

"Sweetheart, why don't you just tell me what Carl did and I'll help you figure out what he needs to be charged with," Robert suggested, his tone so reasonable and calm that it made me even more angry for some reason.

You're not mad at Robert, I told myself as I closed my eyes and took a few deep breaths. I realized I'd been clenching my fists, so I forced my hands open and wiggled my fingers.

I opened my eyes and looked at Robert, touched by the concern on his face. The poor man probably thought I was about to explode. My blood pressure was probably high enough that it might actually be a possibility.

"He... he wouldn't let Elle see a doctor," I started, then turned to pace again. "She needed treatment, but Carl refused to let her go."

"Why didn't she just go anyway?"

An understandable question. We weren't living in the nineteenth century, for cripe's sake. Women had every right a man did. But Robert didn't know the whole story.

"That son of a motherless goat was the only one working, something he insisted on," I explained. Robert sucked in his lips, and I had to assume it was due to my "curse" word.

"He told Elle that since he paid for the health insurance, he didn't want her 'jacking up the rates with her condition'," I sneered with air quotes. Gracious, I was so angry I think I could have actually put my fist through a wall.

"And if she'd gotten treatment when she first found out, then maybe…" My voice trailed off. I couldn't say the words that swarmed around in my head, buzzing like angry insects.

"I want him charged," I repeated instead.

Robert stared at me for a moment, then patted the sofa cushion next to him. My shoulders slumped as I moved around the coffee table and sat. I was at the tail end of my tirade and felt a bit worn out. And defeated.

He slid his arm over my shoulders. "I'm not sure what crime Carl's committed," he said.

"Attempted murder," I suggested.

Robert stiffened and leaned forward slightly to look at me. I barely glanced at him, not wanting to meet his eyes. If I saw any sympathy, I was going to lose my tenuous and questionable hold on my emotions.

"Elle has advanced metastatic bladder cancer," I whispered. "They can't treat it. It's too far gone. She's known about it for a year and Carl never let her get treatment," I gritted out as my hands clenched again. They ached to be around Carl's neck.

"It was Jasmin who insisted they leave Carl and move here," I continued. "Elle said she bullied her into it once Elle admitted what was wrong. I guess Jazz was hoping her mom would be happier here, more comfortable…" I swallowed the rest of the words back.

While she dies.

"Jazz also insisted her mom see a doctor. They sold the piece of junk car Elle had just to pay the oncologist's bill. But they told Elle there wasn't anything they could do." I forced my head to turn so I could look at Robert. His face became blurry as my eyes filled.

"My baby has less than a few months to live," I wailed. Robert murmured something and wrapped both arms around me while I fell apart.

All those wasted years, just gone. All that time I could have had a relationship with my daughter... blown away like dandelion fluff. Once she'd come back home, I'd had such high hopes that we'd be able to rebuild those bridges and to take back some of that lost time.

And now it was too late.

I have no idea how long I cried on Robert, but I was completely worn out by the time I pushed back. The tears had finally subsided, leaving me with dry, aching eyes that felt puffy and difficult to hold open. I didn't bother to try.

"I'll make us some coffee," Robert murmured. I nodded, though I didn't open my eyes.

It was moments later when he returned with two steaming cups. I blinked a few times, trying to force the fog away as I reached out to take the mug he held to me.

I took a sip. "Did you already have some made?" Though it was the same coffee we had at the bakery, for some reason it tasted better, like it was somehow soothing me and my jangled nerves.

He shook his head. "No, I just brewed it."

I frowned; I must have fallen asleep, which was somewhat surprising considering how my mind was still racing.

"Nothing's changed," I muttered as I took another sip. "I still want that jerk charged with... something."

I expected an argument, a "There wasn't a crime committed," lecture. So, I was a little shocked when Robert nodded.

"I'll look into it," he promised. "I have a few criminal attorney friends I'll talk to as well."

That made me smile, though it wasn't easy with my swollen face. Something tickled my foot then and I looked down, surprised to see Wally.

"He came over here as soon as you started crying," Robert said softly. "Poor boy didn't like seeing his mama so upset."

I was amazed I still had any moisture left in my body, but my vision blurred again, and I reached down to scratch Wally's head. "Mama's good boy," I whispered. Wally gave me a grin, though even his looked a little off.

Robert and I made plans for dinner later in the week, and after having him promise to stop by the bakery in the morning, we said our goodbyes and Wally and I headed home.

Jasmin was watching television with Maggie when we walked in. Wally made straight for the girls' bedroom, then sat outside the closed door whining, so Jasmin got up to let him go visit Elle. I wondered if it would do her some good, at least offer comfort.

I could see Maggie staring at me in my peripherals. I knew she could tell something was wrong, but I shook my head slightly. "I'll tell you tomorrow," I promised. "I'm just too drained emotionally right now to discuss it." Thankfully, she let it go and we immersed ourselves in seventies sitcoms. After a few shows, I did feel a bit better.

Maybe there was something to be said about laughter being the best medicine.

"HE'S OUT ON a run," Jasmin said when I asked her where

James was the next afternoon. I needed the kid to get something off the top shelf. Sometimes being short was a real pain in the keester.

I was still feeling the effects of the emotional drama from the day before but was trying to shake it off. Staying busy helped. That, and the talk I'd had with Jasmin and Maggie that morning.

I'd told them what Elle had shared and apologized to Jasmin for wanting to run her father up a flagpole using his intestines. She'd grimaced.

"Gross, Gramma," she'd chuckled. "But honestly, if I didn't have a weak stomach, I'd be right there helping you. I never want to talk to that man again."

It surprised me to hear; Jasmin had always adored her father, at least when she'd been younger. But I suppose once she grew up, she could see him for the manipulative, controlling jerk that he truly was. *Look up Narcissist in the dictionary and you'll see Carl's picture.*

Maggie had another surprisingly good idea, suggesting that we get Elle a home nurse, which morphed into checking into palliative care when Jasmin said her research on metastatic bladder cancer had revealed the patients could suffer from intense pain in the end. I certainly wasn't going to have my daughter go through that, not if I could do something to help.

Todd walked in then, and I smiled slightly. *Thank You Lord, for the distractions.* He certainly knew I needed them.

Jasmin came out of the back room then, carrying the bowl I'd wanted. Her face lit up when she saw Todd, though I drew her attention back to me.

"How in the world did you get that down?"

She shrugged as she placed the bowl on the back counter. "Climbed the shelves."

"Jasmin Elain," I growled, "those shelves are not sturdy! You could have been hurt!"

She waved a dismissive hand as she pulled a mug off the

shelf and poured Todd a cup of coffee. "It's not that high."

I watched as she added a liberal amount of cream, along with several hefty scoops of sugar. I always teased the young contractor that he drank candy, not coffee.

"Sounds like something I better check out," Todd grinned at my granddaughter, though it seemed a little more like a leer to me. Of course, I was looking at him through the protective grandmother lenses, so I had to hold my tongue.

"Maybe I could at least attach those shelves to the wall," he suggested. He took a sip of coffee, grunted appreciatively, then looked at me. "So, Miss Maddie, what are you thinking?"

I poured my own mug, then motioned toward a table and called for Maggie to come join us. She was sitting with Nando and Alice, chatting about Maggie's new role in the upcoming play. It made my back teeth ache to keep from commenting on the fact that Maggie hadn't even had a call from that Angelina person about rehearsals, yet the play was supposed to open in a few months.

I still had suspicions that Angelina had hit Maggie up for a "contribution" to the project.

Once we were all seated, Maggie and I explained the idea for the pet cafe. Todd thought it was a great idea.

"We could probably do some sort of connecting window," he suggested. "Like a carry-out window. That way, people wouldn't have to leave their pets unattended while they came in here to place their order."

"Oh, that's a great idea!" I said. "But first, we have to talk to the shop owners to see if we can cut a hole in the wall." That made Todd laugh.

"Thought you were buying it, like the bakery."

I shook my head. "No, it's just for lease. Not sure if we'd have the money to buy it anyway," I shrugged. Especially not with Elle's medical expenses. Of course, I had no idea how much money that was going to entail. We needed to get her to a doctor first.

After Todd left with the promise he'd talk to the shop owners, James returned from his runs and Jasmin insisted we take Nando and Alice home. "If they eat any more donuts, they're going to go into a sugar coma," she laughed. Jasmin was right; those two old crones could eat a dozen donuts each if we let them.

"Why don't you just take the rest of the day off," Jasmin suggested. "It's slow today with the boat show going on, and James will be here to help." The boy practically strutted like a rooster at that.

I was still worn out enough that it didn't take much encouragement to get me to leave, but once we dropped Nando and Alice off, I asked Maggie if she would mind driving to Floydsville. That earned me some raised brows, which was understandable since I hated going into the city during the week. The traffic was a nightmare.

"I want to go to the library," I explained. "They have the current and recent newspapers there. I just want to check out the articles and see if something clicks about Allen's death." I had no answers so far.

"We have a library here," Maggie protested as she reached for her purse in the backseat. "Or you can read them on the app—"

"No," I shook my head. "I want to read the actual newspaper. And I don't want to go to our library, because word might get around what we're looking for."

Of course, I could bribe Lacy, our young librarian, with lattes and Macon Bacon donuts, but I just wanted to get away. And I didn't feel like explaining to Maggie that I really wasn't ready to walk in the house just yet, though I had guilt over that. Elle could probably use some company, though I had no doubts Wally was with her. I'll spend some time with her when we get back, I told myself, and as much time as I can the next few months. Honestly, though, I was really dreading it.

Watching my only child die was going to be the hardest thing I've ever done.

"Okay," Maggie sighed, unaware of my inner turmoil, "but you can't yell at me about my driving." She lifted her chin, as if to say she meant business.

"Fine," I sighed, though I wasn't promising anything.

THE LIBRARY IN Floydsville was huge, though I doubted it rivaled those in the larger cities. It took a bit of wandering around before we found the local newspapers.

"They have them on the computer, too," a young man told us when we sat at a table and started reading. I looked up at him and read his name tag.

"Thank you, uh, Lukiss." What a ridiculous way to spell that name. "If we need help, we'll ask."

"Where was he when we wandered around the library for the last fifteen minutes?" I muttered.

"What was that?" Maggie asked as she dug around in her purse, then pulled out a pen.

I frowned. "What are you doing with that?" I asked by way of an answer.

Maggie did a little happy dance in her chair as she stared at the page before her. "Word search."

"You can't do the word search in the library's newspaper!" I snapped. She looked up then, a pout starting. I put my hand up to stop whatever argument she was going to give me. "Just... just read the articles and see if anything suspicious jumps out at you."

"Fine," she muttered, putting her pen back in her purse. "Party pooper."

Ignoring her, I skimmed through the headlines for the Crown Hill Chronicle from three weeks prior. There wasn't much by way of news for the area, not even in Floydsville. The usual summer news stories—tourists injured, car break-ins at the beach, drunken brawls—but not much else. I set the paper aside and picked up the following week's.

"Here's something!" Maggie announced. I glanced up. She was holding the Floydsville Flyer, which was a twice-weekly publication, unlike the Chronicle. The Flyer was probably three times as thick as the Chronicle as well.

"What?"

She pointed to the article, like I could see it from across the table. "Read it to me!" I bit out.

"'Janelle Eisenberg, age thirty-seven, was arrested Monday night for trespass. Ms. Eisenberg was found wandering through the Floydsville Cemetery grounds sometime before midnight. When questioned, Ms. Eisenberg claimed to have no memory of why she was there.'"

I stared at her for a moment, waiting for more, but Maggie never looked my way and seemed to be reading a different article.

"And?"

Maggie looked up at me. "Hmm?"

I huffed out a breath. "What else is there to that Eisenberg woman's story? How does it relate to Allen's case."

Her eyebrows pinched in the middle. "It doesn't." She looked back down.

"Then why in the Sam hill did you read it to me?" I said far too loudly. Someone nearby shushed me, and I huffed out a sigh.

Maggie shrugged as she went back to reading whatever had caught her attention. "You said to find something suspicious."

It took several deep breaths to get my blood pressure back down. "And why is some woman who was probably sleepwalking in a cemetery suspicious?"

Maggie looked up and gave me a look that said she thought I was out of touch with things. "She was in a cemetery at night... she's likely either a ghost, a ghoul or a zombie."

I recently saw a commercial on television with a robot who growled, "Frustration loading" then shot laser beams out of his eyes, frying a computer. Sitting across from a happily humming, completely oblivious Maggie, I really, really wanted eyeball laser beams.

More deep breaths were needed. "Just look for something that might be a clue to Allen's death." Honestly, I had no idea what I was looking for either, but I guess I just hoped something would jump out at me.

We sat quietly, poring over the newspapers for a long while when Maggie finally spoke again.

"Oh, look at this," she said as she picked up the paper before her and turned it around to push it across the table. I saw that she had a copy of the Crown Hill Chronicle from five weeks earlier. She leaned over and pointed at a brief paragraph in the "Community News" section.

A famous author who wishes to remain anonymous is going to be visiting our beautiful town! We might not be able to say who it is but be on the lookout for an unfamiliar face... you might just get a chance to chat with a celebrity!

"Huh," I muttered. "Not much of a clue, but I suppose it's better than nothing."

Maggie looked confused again. "Clue?" She leaned a little closer and squinted. "Oh, no, over here," she said, pointing just to the left of the Community News section. "That's what I was trying to show you."

I frowned. "The Lost Pets section?"

She nodded. "Yeah. Look at the third one down. 'Lost orange tabby, female, white tipped tail and black spot on her tongue. Microchipped.'"

I don't know what was more impressive—that Maggie could read upside down, or that she hadn't tipped over from her chest weight and face planted in the table.

"What does that have to do—"

"That's an exact description of Bixby!" she exclaimed. The

136

shusher shushed again. Maggie looked chastised, then sat back down.

"That description fits half the cats in this town," I argued. "Heck, it fits half the cats in our house!" It was true; three of Maggie's cats were orange tabbies and at least one had white on his tail.

She shook her head. "No, the black spot on her tongue is the giveaway. It's unusual in cats, but Bixby has one." A frown creased her brow again. "And that's another thing—Bixby doesn't answer to her name. I call and call her, but she just ignores me. At first, I thought she was deaf, but she's startled a couple of times whenever there was a loud noise. I'm starting to think that's not her name."

I shrugged. "So, maybe Allen found the cat and claimed her as his own."

"No, he specifically said he'd gotten her as a kitten, rescued her from a gas station. He was quite fond of her..." Maggie's eyes narrowed.

"What?" I asked, though I really didn't care. The cat had nothing to do with our investigation and I continued reading through the articles.

"Bixby didn't seem to like Allen much," she said. "She scratched him when he tried to pet her goodbye."

"Maybe she was mad at him for being left." I was distracted by an article about the dangers of Heron Hill, the road leading up to Todd's cabins. Robert had already told me about the accidents, but I didn't realize there had been so many. In the past few months, three bicyclists and two pedestrians had been hit or nearly hit by passing cars.

Maggie was going on about how sweet Bixby was and how she got along with the other cats, but still kept trying to get out of the window, but I only half-listened.

After a little while, my neck started to ache from hunching over the table, so I sat back. Maggie was copying some recipe she'd found, which irritated me, since she was doing absolutely zero to help find clues. I sighed as I stretched, but as I did so, something caught my eye from the newspaper Maggie had set aside. I pulled it toward me.

It was a short blurb, hardly noticeable, about a woman who was looking for her missing husband. The middle sentence drew my attention. *Mrs. Oberlander and her husband had been on vacation in Crown Hill when Mr. Jerome T. Oberlander, 48, left their rental home Thursday to pick up a food order. He never returned and the couple's car was found abandoned on Pelican Lane. Mrs. Oberlander is asking...*

Something about the article pricked at my memory, but I couldn't quite grasp it. Knowing it would take days to go through all the newspapers again to look for anything relating to the Oberlander's, I instead left Maggie and went in search of Lukiss, then asked the kid if he could do a search on the computer.

"Of course!" he said with far too much enthusiasm as he sat in front of one of the public computers, fingers flying over the keyboard when I gave him the name I was looking for.

"I've been considering teaching a technology class for the elderly," he said while I ignored his comment and watched while he brought up a string of articles. Well, that's certainly handy. In just seconds, he found four different articles in the area newspapers about the missing man.

"My heart just goes out to you elderly who have no clue what's going on in today's world," Lukiss went on. If the kid was trying to get on my good side, he was failing miserably. Those laser eyeball beams came to mind again. That's some technology I'd sure embrace, I thought to myself.

He looked at me over his shoulder, the light catching on the ring through his eyebrow. I wondered how much it would hurt if I yanked on it. The kid gave me a sympathetic smile.

"You all are just so lost—"

"Can you print those articles?" I interrupted. If he mentioned one more time how the "elderly" were out of touch with technology, I was going to pit Maggie against him in a Candy Crush Saga match. The woman played that game on her phone every chance she got.

I waited impatiently while Lukiss retrieved the sheets of paper from the printer. I was onto something, I was sure of it, though I wasn't sure how to tie it all together. But something had caught my eye in one of the articles I'd read over Lukiss's shoulder... Missus Oberlander's first name was Brandy. And I'd suddenly remembered the wedding ring I'd found in Allen's cabin.

But the question was—why would some tourist kill Allen and then disappear?

Chapter 14

MY MIND WAS reeling as Maggie drove us back to Crown Hill. There were so many questions that needed answers... and I wasn't finding those answers. I was starting to question my ability to solve a crime, though I knew I couldn't possibly have been as bad as Jonny at it.

"Today's the longest day of the year," Maggie said, bringing me out of my thoughts. I glanced at the sun, surprised at how low it was on the horizon. The clock on the dash said it was seven-thirty-three.

"We need to decide if we're going to be open for the fourth of July," she went on. "It's on a Wednesday this year. I'd like to close, but the parade is going right down Sandpiper. Jason at the town hall said it was going to start at the bank and end at the deli just past the bakery. I think we could make out like pandas, selling pastries to parade watchers!"

"Bandits," I corrected her absently, my mind on all the hows and whys of the case. If that Oberlander fellow's car had been abandoned, did that mean he'd run out of gas or something? And did Allen give him a ride? If so, what in the world happened to make the man kill Allen? But even more strangely—how did Oberlander lose his wedding ring?

"Bandits?" Maggie laughed. "That makes no sense. Why would bandits kiss?"

I whipped my head toward her. "What are you talking about?"

She scrunched her mouth to the side as she looked at me. "Watch the road!" I admonished.

Maggie jerked the wheel to the left, getting us back on the road, but not before she clipped a mile marker sign with her front bumper. It was a wonder her car wasn't completely banged up.

"I was just questioning why you'd think the expression was

'make out like bandits'," she said, rolling her eyes. "That's dumb. It has to be pandas, because I can't imagine bandits kissing. They're all about violence, not love."

I frowned. "Are you stu... never mind," I shook my head, glad I'd managed to stop from saying what I was really thinking. "It's not making out like kissing; it's making out, like getting a good deal. You know, a steal."

Maggie huffed. "That's dumb. I like the idea of happy pandas kissing better."

I sighed. "Whatever." There was no point in arguing with the woman. Her brain just didn't work like most others.

"Maybe we could sell sno-cones too," she went on, though I was barely paying attention. "Even though the parade is in the morning, it's going to be hot. Remember last year when Hope passed out? I didn't think the fire department..."

I tuned her out completely when she started talking about how strong the EMTs were. Maggie was incurably man crazy. Any male drew her attention like a moth to a candle flame. *All but Edwin...*

That took my mind back to the man who'd seemed a likely suspect at first. There were an awful lot of clues pointing at him, but things never seemed to add up just right. For one, that cigar ash... Edwin claimed he hadn't smoked in a year. Plus, I couldn't imagine someone lighting a person on fire while casually smoking. But then, I wasn't a murderer, so who knew?

Then there was the laptop with the screens conveniently opened to Edwin's web page, as well as the Crown Hill PD. And the signed book from Edwin...

"...sell some more of those red, white and blue cupcakes," Maggie went on. "Except people complained about their lips turning blue. But maybe we could make that a selling point, you know, like 'Eat M&M's cupcakes and look like one of the walking dead!'"

"Mm hmm," I murmured noncommittally. Robert had also mentioned finding a lighter near the body, which I had forgotten about. I would just about give my right kidney betting that the lighter belonged to Edwin and had his fingerprints all over it. Except I was almost one hundred percent certain Edwin hadn't killed Allen.

And I was almost just as certain someone was trying to frame Edwin. But who and why?

"...coffee and hot cocoa, but it's going to be so hot. Maybe we can just make iced coffee. I bet that would be popular! But is there such a thing as iced hot cocoa?"

"Chocolate milk," I muttered as I stared out the window. Why would someone want to frame Edwin? I continued to question. A disgruntled fan? There was that recent book where he killed off the favorite protagonist. Maybe he ticked someone off. I mentally rolled my eyes. Oh, heck, now I'm starting to sound like Maggie!

"Oh yeah, duh," Maggie laughed. From the corner of my eye, I saw her turn toward me. "Well, we really should look into getting a soda machine. Not everyone wants hot drinks with their..."

Edwin didn't mention his lighter was missing, though. But then, why would he? It's not like he's a good friend. *Maybe he didn't even notice it was missing anyway, if he's not smoking any longer...*

"...I could offer my big rack."

That caught my attention, and I whipped my head around to frown at Maggie. "What?" I didn't want to admit I hadn't been paying attention, but I had to know what she was talking about.

Her lips pursed as she signaled to turn onto our street. "Weren't you paying any attention to me at all? I said, the Methodist church is having a big community yard sale and invited all the other churches to join them. Pastor Winchester talked about it Sunday; don't you remember?"

I didn't, mostly because he'd droned on and on about how God doesn't have a retirement plan and we're all supposed to keep doing His work until the worms come and chew on our bones. Something like that. I was fairly certain the sermon had been directed at me, since Winchester was feeling the effects of my dropping out of so many committees.

"Anyway, I was thinking about donating that huge set of deer horns I have. You know, the one my daddy hunted back in Georgia and had mounted." She pulled into the driveway and shut the car off.

"They're antlers, not horns," I told her as we climbed out of the car. Both of us moaned. It had been a long day and I wanted a long soak in some hot, bubbly water.

"Whatever," Maggie huffed. Jasmin had borrowed my car to get to work and I saw that it was in the drive. I winced, knowing I'd put off talking to Elle all day. *Guess the bath will have to wait.*

"But men love a big rack," Maggie repeated just as we walked in. Jasmin was sitting on the sofa, and I nearly tripped over my feet when I saw Edwin sitting next to her. The grumpy man was grinning, likely at Maggie's comment.

"We do, that's for sure," he said. Maggie giggled as she waved and announced she was going to check on "the girls."

"What are you doing here?" I blurted to Edwin, then shook my head. "Sorry, I didn't mean that to be rude. I, uh, just didn't see a car." And how in the world did he know where we lived?

Edwin waved his hand in a dismissive manner, but it was Jasmin who answered. "Mister Evans came by the bakery this afternoon. We got to talking and I invited him to dinner." My granddaughter widened her eyes with a grin, begging me not to argue.

I laughed. "Are you cooking, sweetheart?" Jasmin could burn water if anyone let her into the kitchen, which we most certainly did not. She might be showing a lot of talent for cake decorating, but only after someone else did the baking.

"Gramma—" She started to protest, but I held up my hand.

"I was kidding. We hadn't really planned for anything fancy," I told my author hero. "But you're welcome to the meatloaf I was going to make." I hadn't been planning on cooking at all since there were plenty of leftovers, but I certainly couldn't serve company warmed over linguine.

"I love meatloaf," Edwin said with a semblance of a smile. I realized we had a lot in common; the resting grouch face was a real thing. Most people thought I was a grump and... well, truthfully, they probably weren't wrong.

Maybe I needed to change my attitude.

I headed in the kitchen and fixed a tray with iced tea and lemonade. "Hope you weren't expecting alcohol," I said as I set the tray on the coffee table. "This is a dry house."

Edwin laughed. "You mean whiskey?" He shook his head. "Not all authors are drinkers. Silly stereotype."

I smirked as I handed him a glass full of ice, watching as he helped himself to the lemonade. "Well, so is cigar smoking."

That earned me a snort as the man sat back. "That is true." He glanced at me. "I, uh, gave up the bourbon when I gave up the smoking."

I couldn't help the laugh that escaped me. Jasmin seemed a bit lost at our conversation, so I bent over to pat her knee.

"Gonna go talk to your mama," I told her, then looked at Edwin with a grimace. "I don't mean to be rude, but... well, I'll let Jasmin explain." I don't know why I felt the need to explain our personal lives to the man, but for some reason, I did.

"Maggie will be out in a few, after she checks on her cats," I said.

Edwin grinned. "I love cats," he admitted. "Always said if I'd been born female, I woulda been a cat lady."

For some reason, that made me laugh again. I was still shaking my head when I walked down the hall to Elle's room. The door was open, so I didn't bother announcing myself when I walked in.

Wally was on the bed, curled up next to Elle. It made me smile to see the sweet boy offering what comfort he could to my daughter. I had to swallow hard at all the emotion trying to crawl its way up my throat.

Elle's eyes were closed, but I had the impression she wasn't asleep. I realized she had nothing to do in the room, and if she was going to be bedridden, then I wanted her to be as comfortable as possible. Some books, maybe. A television. Maybe a laptop. *I need to talk to Robert.*

The realization that my mind instantly went to Robert with all my problems startled me. I'd been a widow for over five years and had done fine on my own. Robert and I had just been "dating" for a few weeks, yet he'd become so important to me that I thought I needed to include him in all my decision making.

I wasn't sure how I felt about that.

"How are you doing?" I said softly as I sat next to Elle. Wally lifted his head at the sound of my voice, and I reached over her to scratch him behind his ears.

"Mmkay," Elle mumbled. I grimaced when I saw that she looked worse. Much worse. It was shocking how much she'd deteriorated in the handful of weeks since she and Jasmin had arrived. I swallowed hard at the tears threatening to form as I once again cursed the years we'd lost.

"We have a nurse practitioner scheduled to come tomorrow," I told her in case Jasmin hadn't. "She's a pain specialist, so she should be able to help make you comfortable." I choked on the rest of the words... *Since there's nothing else we can do.*

I blinked rapidly and cleared my throat.

"Not in pain," Elle whispered. "Not really. Just... so... tired." She didn't need to tell me that, since she hadn't even opened her eyes once so far. "Won't be long..."

There was no point in trying to stop the tears from flowing then. Elle didn't have the strength to even open her eyes to witness her mother falling apart. I ran a shaking hand over her head, grimacing at the greasy feel and sour smell coming from her body. I'd make a note to ask the nurse if she could bathe Elle. We'd do whatever it took to make my girl as comfortable as possible.

145

Another throat clearing was required before I could speak again. "Well, I'll let you rest." I stood and Wally lifted his head to look at me with a forlorn expression. I wondered if he understood what was happening. It was likely; the dog was far too intelligent.

Maggie was in the living room, chatting. I was thankful for that, because I wasn't ready to pretend everything was okay when it certainly wasn't. My face must have revealed too much of the heartbreak I was feeling, because Jasmin jumped up and ran over to wrap her arms around me.

"Oh, Gramma, I know," she murmured, her voice catching on her words. "It's hard. It's so hard." She sniffled then, pushed back to look at me. I was always amazed at how much taller the girl was than me; in my mind, the memory of her as a young child in braids with a chocolate ring around her mouth lingered.

"At least she's not suffering," Jasmin shrugged. We both knew it was a small victory in the fight against a life-stealing disease that we had no defense against. Still, I nodded and patted her arm. I glanced at Maggie and Edwin, who'd grown quiet as they watched us, not even bothering to pretend they weren't eavesdropping. I tried to smile.

"I'll go start dinner," I croaked, then headed into the kitchen as I heard Edwin mumble that he should go. Both Jasmin and Maggie protested.

There was a small comfort in the routine of cracking eggs and measuring spices, chopping onion and bell pepper, though my mind kept returning to the woman down the hall I wouldn't have recognized if I'd run into her on the street. After slicing my finger thanks to my blurred vision, I forced my mind to concentrate on Allen's case instead.

The question of why someone might want to frame Edwin for the death still lingered. Did they plan to murder Allen and frame Edwin? Or was it just a coincidence that it was Allen who became the victim? And what about his car... did that Oberlander fellow drive Allen's car for some reason and hit Allen?

I sighed; I needed to let Robert know I had the wedding ring, because it was obviously evidence. I wasn't looking forward to that conversation, and I played it out in my mind as I rolled out the cracker crumbs for the meatloaf.

"You took this from the crime scene?" Robert would say indignantly. "That's tampering!"

I'd give him a look haughty enough to make him cringe. "Well, if the police officers," I'd say with air quotes to make my point, "would have done their job properly, then they would have found that important piece of evidence, right?"

I imagined Robert not having a rebuttal for that.

Mixing the ingredients with more force than was probably necessary, I laughed to myself at my imaginings. "You're a ridiculous old woman," I muttered out loud.

"That's not very nice!" Maggie said from behind me, making me jump. "And what did I do this time?"

I glanced at her over my shoulder and saw her open the fridge. "Grab a stick of butter, would you?" I asked.

She pulled out a bottle of juice and handed me the butter. "Thanks. I wasn't talking about you, by the way."

"Then—"

"I was talking to myself," I said a bit snappishly, then sighed. "Sorry, I don't mean to lash out at you. I'm just… stressed." Even as the words left me, I felt the tension in my shoulders and rolled my head around. I jumped when I felt Maggie's arms go around me from behind.

"I'm so sorry," she whispered. "We'll do everything we can for Elle. Any money I have is yours. We'll get her the best care, I promise."

"Oh, honey," I sobbed as I turned to hug her back, careful to not get my greasy hands on her blouse. "Thank you. Thank you." The generous offer was worth a repeat of my gratitude.

"Am I interrupting something?"

We separated and looked at Edwin. Both of us had tears

147

running down our cheeks and I huffed out a laugh as I used the crook of my arm to wipe my face, then turned to finish patting the loaf in the pan.

"Sorry," Maggie told the man. "I got distracted." I sniffled while I heard ice being dispensed from the refrigerator, then liquid being poured.

"Ah," Edwin said a moment later. "Thank you. My blood sugar was about to take a dive."

"Diabetes?" I asked, though I didn't turn. The meatloaf was ready for the oven, so I slid it in and set the timer. Normally, I would have made homemade mashed potatoes for company, but instant was going to have to do, because I was in no mood to peel a half dozen spuds. I moved to the sink to wash my hands.

"Type 2," Edwin answered. "I've gone too long without eating. Get the shakes and a bit dizzy when I do that."

"Oh no," Maggie fussed. "Sit down." I watched as she led the man to the kitchen table and even pulled out a chair for him. The laugh escaped me before I could stop it when she put the back of her hand to his forehead.

"You don't run a fever when you have diabetes," I chuckled. Maggie looked embarrassed and I felt bad for a moment. I grabbed the package of crackers I'd opened for the meatloaf and headed to the table.

"Here," I said as I placed them before Edwin. "Dinner won't be ready for an hour or so. Want some cheese?"

He shook his head as he nibbled at a cracker. The man looked a bit more frail than he had when we'd first met him and I realized there was no way he could have killed Allen. Well, I supposed he could have hit him with the car, but there was no way he could have dragged his body into the house.

The thought made me remember one of my questions. "Edwin, are you missing a lighter by chance?"

That question drew his brows together. "I am," he nodded. "It was a gift from my agent when I sold my first million books."

He eyeballed me a bit suspiciously. "How did you know?"

I ignored the question. "When did you misplace it?"

The eyeballing continued. "'Spose a few months ago," he said. "Maybe less."

I nodded. "After you got here?"

He set his cracker down. "Why are you asking?"

A heavy sigh left me as I pursed my lips. "I'm asking because I think someone is framing you for the murder of Allen Rogers."

Chapter 15

DINNER WAS pleasant. Edwin went on and on about how amazing my meatloaf was, which caused me to blush because I could tell he was being sincere.

"You need to come back tomorrow for a meatloaf sandwich," Maggie'd told the man. "She makes them with the leftovers and they're the best!"

"Only if I use your incredible homemade sourdough bread," I'd argued, making Maggie grin.

Jasmin had rolled her eyes at us. "Enough with the brown-nosing. Everyone knows you're both great in the kitchen. It'd be nice if you'd impart some of your culinary wisdom to the third generation over here. I'm only known for my mean microwave ramen skills."

Through our conversations, I found out Edwin suspected Allen followed him to our town once he found out Edwin was going to be there. I fully expected Maggie to come to Allen's defense, but was surprised when she not only kept quiet, but seemed overly attentive to Edwin. Like a mother hen with her chicks, she fussed and fawned over the man to the point it was almost embarrassing.

Edwin had said his agent was the only one who knew exactly where he was going to be over the course of the summer, but since I knew he and Allen had the same agent, it wasn't a far stretch to believe that Allen had somehow found out where Edwin would be. More and more I believed Edwin was being framed.

But I still had no idea who.

"Is it at all possible your agent would want you framed for murder?" I asked as I helped myself to another serving of potatoes. I had to admit, the new instant potatoes weren't bad at all; not like they used to be back when I was a newly married homemaker. Then, wallpaper paste tasted better than the instant potatoes.

Edwin laughed hard enough that he choked on his food. Maggie was on the man in an instant, pounding on his back so hard I thought she might break a rib.

"If he's coughing, don't pound on him!" I hollered. Edwin continued to cough, but he managed to reach out and squeeze Maggie's hand when she made her way back to her chair. It was such a banal gesture, but the woman blushed like he'd dipped her over his arm and laid one on her.

Once Edwin cleared his throat, he grinned at me. "Eloise wouldn't hurt a fly," he said. "She's almost as old as us, for one thing; for another, she gets a hefty commission on my book sales. She's made millions."

That shot that theory in the foot. "Is there anyone else you can think of who would want to harm you?" I was starting to sound like Jonny with his lame questions, but I was at a loss to figure it out. Maybe I wasn't such a good detective after all.

For the tenth time in an hour, I sighed, not knowing the questions to ask. Edwin saved me.

"Surely there isn't just the lighter as evidence," he said. "Did the cops find anything else?"

"They never find anything," Maggie supplied. "They're definitely not *Hawaii 5-0*." I grinned at her.

"I found a cigar ash on the floor in the living room of the cabin," I answered. "There was also one of your books, a signed copy, conveniently sitting on the table. And Allen's laptop was there, no password or anything. The... that thing where you search for stuff—"

"It's a browser, Gramma," Jasmin laughed. I nodded.

"Yeah, the browser thingy," I said with a wave. Jasmin laughed harder, shaking her head. "It was open to your website, as well as Dickie—er, Richard Thompson, Crown Hill's police chief. I also found what I figured was Allen's latest manuscript." I pinched my lips from saying what I was thinking.

Edwin chuckled as he chewed. When he swallowed, he

pointed his fork at me. "From the look on your face, I can tell you weren't impressed."

I shook my head. "It's not kind to speak ill of the dead, but... no, I was not impressed. His writing is... uh, was..."

"Mediocre?" Edwin supplied. "Juvenile? Contrived?"

I laughed. "All of the above. But it was a little strange that the program was open to a section where he was writing about someone who was burned beyond recognition. Almost too much of a coincidence, if you ask me."

Edwin made a contemplative sound while Maggie gasped, drawing our attention. She'd been quiet up to that point. "Allen predicted his own death? I had no idea he was a psycho!"

Jasmin laughed, obviously thinking she was kidding. I gave my granddaughter a look and a head shake. She's not joking. Jasmin bit her lips to keep from laughing further.

"Psychic," I corrected. "Anyway," I went on with a look at Maggie that said I thought she was a fork shy of a place setting, "it all screams 'set up' to me."

Edwin nodded. "Yeah," he agreed, "but it also screams bad novel," he laughed. "I couldn't have written anything this contrived."

I smiled. "Well, regardless, I'm sure the Crown Hill PD is going to figure things out soon enough and come looking for you."

He shrugged. "Ain't got anything to hide," he said nonchalantly, his Texas drawl more pronounced. I wondered if he felt as tired as he looked. "The evidence will prove my innocence."

I smiled at him, though it was forced. I hoped Edwin was right, but I was really having my doubts... especially about Jonny's ability to figure things out.

After Edwin left, insisting he "take an Uber," whatever in the world that meant, rather than having Jasmin drive him back to the bakery where he'd left his car, I made my excuses and left Maggie and Jasmin cleaning the kitchen while I headed to my room to take a bath.

And to call Robert.

As predicted, the man was not happy that I'd taken evidence. He'd ranted for a full two minutes before I interrupted him.

"It technically wasn't a crime scene when I found the ring," I reminded him. "Your grandson had decided that Allen had accidentally caught himself on fire, remember? Really, all I'm guilty of is finder's keeper's."

That made him chuckle, though I could tell it was involuntary. He cleared his throat. "Don't forget breaking and entering when you went in the cabin."

"I didn't break anything. I used a key," I reminded him. "And Todd would be the one to have to press charges, which we both know he isn't going to do." The young man had become a pretty good friend, but the fact that Maggie and I had just agreed to pay him another eight thousand to convert the shop next door for our pet bakery just cemented my argument.

Robert sighed and I waited for him to realize there wasn't anything he could really gripe about. My bath water was growing cold, so I reached over and turned the hot faucet on.

"Is that water?" Robert asked. "Wait... are you taking a bath right now?" His voice was higher than usual as he asked the question.

"Yeah," I told him as I sighed in relief when the warm water poured over my feet. I loved baths, but lately hadn't had the time for a good, long soak. "I even added Epsom salts. It feels wonderful on my old achy bones."

Robert coughed a bit, then muttered something about needing to get off the phone. He sounded a bit choked, for some reason.

Almost as soon as I hung up, my phone rang. I grinned, thinking it was Robert, wanting to add something to his argument. *Bring it on, buddy*, I thought to myself. While I enjoyed laughing with the man, I really loved debating with him.

To my surprise, Betty Winchester's name showed on the screen. I had no idea why the pastor's wife would be calling me on a Friday night, but I answered anyway, despite wanting to soak in peace and quiet. I reached over and turned the water off, then answered the phone.

"Hi Betty," I said with less enthusiasm than I should have.

"Maddie!" she trilled. "I'm so glad you answered. Listen, I hate to ask. I mean, I *really* hate to ask, but do you think you could clean the church tomorrow? Two of the cleaning committee members are off on vacation and I broke my stupid wrist today and the doctor says I can't do anything with that hand for at least three weeks." She spoke so fast it took a minute for my brain to catch up. And when it did, I wished it hadn't.

"Sure," I sighed. But then I frowned. "What about Maggie?" She'd said she wanted to continue cleaning the church and had, as far as I knew. Every Saturday she was gone nearly all day.

"Maggie?" Betty said, sounding confused. "She hasn't cleaned the church since you quit. She said she had rehearsals for a play."

That shocked the socks right off me... if I'd been wearing some anyway. "Oh yeah, silly me," I said, instead of admitting Maggie hadn't confided in me. "Well, you can count on me to get it cleaned. Can't guarantee how clean though." Spiteful me planned on leaving a few pieces of lint on the sanctuary carpet, right in front of the pulpit so Pastor Winchester had to stare at them through his sermon.

Shame on me, I thought to myself with just a tiny pinch of guilt. *It's the Lord's house, remember?*

We hung up, then I let the bath water out. It was getting late, but I wanted to have words with Miss Margaret May Connor, demanding to know why she'd led me to believe she was still cleaning the church on Saturdays, when she'd been rehearsing instead.

"I didn't want to tell you, because you just kept badmouthing the play," Maggie whined when I confronted her in the kitchen where she'd been making popcorn.

I filled the tea kettle and set it on the stove. I needed some chamomile tea if I was going to get to sleep. Even the bath hadn't helped relax me, not with my mind on a million different things.

"Well, I'm not going to say anything." *At least not to you.* "You don't need to be a closet thespian." I snickered at my little joke, but Maggie just grinned and nodded.

"Thank you," she gushed. "It's been so hard keeping that from you." Her face fell. "I don't like lying to my best friend."

I smiled back. Maggie might drive me to distraction at times and make me want to shred wallpaper with my teeth whenever she got on one of her "monsters lurking" tangents, but she was a very good person, and I was thankful to have her as a friend.

Once the popcorn and tea were ready, we settled on the sofa to watch a few episodes of *Murder, She Wrote.* While I normally loved watching Jessica Fletcher, aka Angela Lansbury, in crime-solving action, my mind was still off concentrating on other things.

Edwin hadn't offered any suggestion as to how Allen had come by a signed copy of his book. But when I thought about it, the inscription wasn't personal, wasn't written to Allen. It was actually rather rote, as if something he'd written over and over at a book signing. For all I knew, Allen had gone to one of Edwin's signings in disguise.

I should have dug deeper about the missing lighter, like how had it gone missing? Was there a break-in? Did he misplace it, or leave it on a table in a restaurant or something? And while I knew he'd quit smoking a year before, or so he said, did everyone else know that? Was the cigar ash conveniently left on the floor by someone who'd wanted to frame Edwin, but hadn't known he'd quit?

But above all, my thoughts went back to that ring, the one I promised to give to Robert, who said he'd make some excuse to Jonny so I wouldn't get in trouble. *Sweet man, even if he is a liar,* I laughed to myself. At least he was lying for my benefit, but I'd still have to remember to ask the Lord to forgive him when I said my prayers before bed.

Once Jonny had the ring, he might put two-and-two together, although he'd likely come up with five or six. No one had ever accused Jonathon Donovan of being a Mensa candidate. But it was possible he'd figure out the connection to the Oberlanders and I realized I wanted to talk to Brandy Oberlander myself first and planned to find out where she lived and get over there first thing in the morning. And then I remembered I had to clean the church.

A heavy sigh drew Maggie's attention. "Something wrong?" I startled out of my thoughts, surprised to see the show was on a commercial break. I'd been so lost to my musings I'd almost forgotten Maggie was there.

I glanced at her, chuckling when I saw popcorn crumbs on her pajama top, as well as spots of tea. The woman was a bit of a slob. While I wanted to share my thoughts, I didn't want to burden her with the case. From the way her face lit up when she just mentioned the play, I knew it was something she really enjoyed and if I mentioned the case, she'd feel obligated to help me with it. I shook my head.

"No, I'm... just dreading cleaning the church tomorrow," I said instead. It wasn't a lie; once I'd quit the cleaning committee, I'd realized I'd been doing it for all the wrong reasons—recognition; trying to please others; maybe even trying to please God. Having to go back was an irritation, if I could admit such a thing.

"I can tell Angelina that I have to miss—"

"No," I interrupted, "you go to your rehearsal. I'm just being a whiny baby." I gave her a pouty face that made her laugh and lean over to nudge me with her shoulder.

The show came back on, and we both got engrossed in the story. Jessica Fletcher was working hard to solve her stockbroker's murder. It was a good episode and kept my mind off our own case, but my eyes started getting heavy.

The next thing I knew, the sun was just starting to crest the horizon and I was still on the sofa, though I had my bed pillow and my comforter. I smiled when I realized Maggie had taken care of me, and the smile broadened when I smelled coffee.

Murmuring drew me to the kitchen. I was surprised to see Robert sitting at the kitchen table with Maggie and Jasmin, eating scones and drinking coffee. I tightened my robe, even though I was wearing pajamas. Still, I didn't want anything showing.

"Good morning, sleezy head," Maggie chirped. Jasmin spit coffee on the table, Robert choked on his bite, and I glared at Maggie.

"It's sleepy head, goofball," I told her as I poured a cup of coffee, then fixed it the way I liked it.

"Sleepy head?" Maggie asked. "Really?"

I snorted as I stirred my coffee. "Why in the world would you greet someone who just woke up by calling them 'sleezy head'?" I asked as I turned and took the empty chair. Robert served me a slice of scone and I smiled my thanks at him.

It occurred to me I probably looked a mess, but I didn't really care. Robert had seen me in all states when I'd stayed at his house during the troubles with the serial killer. One nice thing about getting old, I thought, no such thing as bad hair days. You had to care what you looked like to have a bad hair day, after all.

Maggie didn't answer my question, but instead put her dishes in the sink and made the excuse that she needed to get to the bakery to put the pastry dough she'd made the day before in the oven so there'd be fresh danishes.

"And then I'm going to rehearsal," she said with a slight smile at me. I nodded as I sipped my coffee.

"You know about that?" Jasmin asked. I looked at her with a lifted eyebrow. Maggie rushed out of the kitchen after the question.

"Surprised Maggie finally told you," Robert added. I gave

them both an exasperated look.

"Why in the world do the two of you know about the play, but I just found out last night?"

Robert and Jasmin shrugged in unison. "You're a bit... high-strung at times, dear," Robert said.

Jasmin nodded. "Yeah, Gramma. You get kinda sideways with Maggie a lot."

I couldn't argue; they were right. Instead, I ate my breakfast and finished my coffee, then tried to talk Robert into helping me clean the church, but he had a meeting with Jonny to give him the ring. I didn't ask what excuse he was going to give his grandson for having it.

After changing clothes and rushing through my morning routine, I gave Wally some love and said my goodbyes with promises of a walk later, then took Jasmin to the bakery on my way to church. There was already a line at the door, which made me laugh.

"Are you sure you don't need help?" I asked. "I can stay and go to the church later."

She shook her head with a smile as she opened the door. My old car door creaked like an old woman. We had a lot in common.

"James is going to be here this morning," she grinned. "We make a good team."

I smiled back as I leaned over to look at her. "It's a shame he's so young. You two would make a cute couple." I expected a lot of denial, but Jasmin just tilted her head at me.

"James is a year and a half younger than me," she said, surprising me. "Not that much younger." Interesting.

The church was surprisingly clean, so I just sterilized the bathrooms and emptied waste cans. And since that had taken so little time, I decided to be nice and vacuumed the sanctuary, though that rotten part of me still wanted to toss some lint on the plush navy carpet.

It wasn't even nine o'clock by the time I was finished, so I made my way to Wanda's real estate office, thankful when I saw her car out front but no others.

"Maddie!" my old high school friend chirped from a desk in the back. I honestly thought she would have retired years before, but Wanda said she had to stay busy, and that she couldn't trust anyone else to handle the business.

She stood with a grin and came to me, giving me a hug. Wanda was a tiny thing, just as she'd been in school when she'd been a cheerleader. She was always the one who was put at the top of the cheerleader pyramid. I always felt a bit like Sasquatch around her, even though I was on the short side myself.

Wanda motioned to a chair opposite her desk. "Coffee?" I nodded, watching as she moved to a coffee bar and poured me a cup. I watched as she fixed it, which made me smile to think she remembered.

Once we were both sipping our coffee, Wanda smiled at me. "What brings you in? You're still planning on taking the Murphy storefront, right?"

I grinned. "Well, considering I contracted with Todd to make the improvements we need, I better be planning on going through with it." I shook my head. "No, I came to ask a favor."

Wanda's smile widened. "Ask away."

I thought about how to ask the woman what I wanted to know. I finally decided the direct route was the best one.

"I need to talk to a woman whose husband has gone missing. She's a tourist—"

"Brandy Oberlander," Wanda interrupted with a nod. My eyebrows rose.

She shrugged. "It's not like Crown Hill has a lot of crime. And it's an unusual last name. When I saw the story on my newspaper app, it caught my eye." Her smile dissolved. "Sad story, having your husband just disappear like that. She's still looking for him, I hear. Been bugging the police, but you know how they are."

"Incompetent?" I suggested with a false grin that made

Wanda laugh, though she nodded.

"Anyway, I'd like to talk to Missus Oberlander. I might have some information that could help her." I lifted a shoulder. "I'm sure you rented to her since you're the only Realtor in town," I laughed, "and I know it's probably not done, and maybe not even legal, but if you could give me her address, I'd really appreciate it. I promise, I only have the best intentions." *Intentions of figuring out how and why her husband was involved in Allen's murder.*

Wanda shook her head slightly. "I can't give you that. It's confidential." My heart sunk a bit, but then she winked at me.

"Did you know that I rented Norton's house? He's up north visiting his kids for the summer. Nice couple rented it, though the man went missing a few weeks back."

I laughed at her sneakiness, then we chatted for a bit, before I made my excuses and headed out to Norton's house. Though it was unlikely Jonny would figure things out from the inscription on the ring, I still wanted to make sure I talked to Brandy first.

It was ten by the time I got there, so I felt safe knocking on the door. I could hear movement inside, then blinked a few times once the door was opened. The woman standing before me looked like she'd been up all night, crying. I swallowed at the sympathy that crawled up my throat, forcing it back down. It was looking mighty suspicious that the woman's husband was a murderer, after all.

"May I help you?" she asked, her voice barely more than a whisper.

I cleared my throat. "Hi, I'm Maddie Kaye. I live here in Crown Hill and…" I puffed out my cheeks as I blew out a breath. I hadn't really thought about what I was going to tell the woman.

She tilted her head and looked like she was about to slam the door in my face, so I just said the first thing that came to mind. "I'm investigating a murder, and I think your husband might have been involved." *Smooth, Madelyn, real smooth.*

160

I was a horrible liar.

Brandy's eyes widened and her hand went to her throat. "You think J.T. was murdered?" she asked as her face paled so much I was afraid she was going to faint.

"No!" I shook my head. "No, sorry. I... uh, I just think he might know something about a murder that took place up on Heron Hill."

Brandy nodded once with a look that was both relieved and disappointed. I heard a car coming and glanced over my shoulder, then looked back at her.

"Do you mind if I come inside so we can talk?" She hesitated for a moment, but then nodded as she stepped aside.

The house was nice, though too busy for my taste. Norton was in his eighties and had lost his wife, Regina, to cancer the year before. Sixty years of marriage had cluttered the house with mementos of a long life.

Despite the congested décor, food wrappers, throwaway cups and used tissues were strewn about. Brandy seemed to notice her surroundings then and hurried to start gathering trash.

"I'm sorry," she said as she scooped food containers off the coffee table, "I haven't been myself—"

"Don't apologize." I stepped over to the end table at the arm of the sofa and gathered the cups that were there, fighting to keep the disgust from my face when I saw the gnats that were crawling about.

"When my husband died, I laid about in my own filth for weeks," I admitted. I winced when she sucked in a breath. "I didn't mean your husband is dead," I rushed on. "I just meant that dealing with tragedy of any kind takes the forefront. Often, we get too wrapped up in our head to deal with the everyday stuff."

Ugh, I'm not exactly philosopher material.

Brandy nodded as she walked to the kitchen to put her armload in the trash. I followed.

"Would you like something to drink?" she asked.

"No, thank you," I said as I dropped the cups in the open can. "Uh, we need to get this outside. Does Norton have a trash bin somewhere?"

Brandy told me where it was after I explained Norton was the homeowner. I'd forgotten that the Oberlanders had rented the place through Wanda's agency.

Once we were back inside and seated in the living room, I explained about Allen's death and how I'd found her husband's wedding ring. I left out the part that it had been under the bed, realizing that bit of information might lead to conclusions I hadn't thought of before.

Was it possible J.T. and Allen had been lovers?

I mentally shook myself and forced my attention back on what Brandy was saying.

"...when he left. I called and called him, but he never answered. I hired an Uber to drive me around, looking for him, but after an hour, I decided to go to the police instead." Her shoulders lifted.

"They weren't much help," she sighed. "But they did find J.T.'s car. I guess he'd run out of gas." Her eyes filled. "He was so scatterbrained," she said with a wobbly smile. "That was probably the tenth time he'd run out of gas."

I noticed she was talking about her husband in the past tense, and figured she'd resigned herself to thinking he was dead. It made me wonder if he might just be.

Could there have been two murders? My pulse kicked up a notch at the possibility of yet another serial killer in our sleep town. *Maybe J.T. ran out of gas and the killer picked him up, then ran over Allen...* Again, I shook the thoughts away. They made no sense, for one thing. The evidence pointed to the fact that Allen had possibly been hit by his own car and I couldn't wrap my mind around how in the world that had happened.

After chatting with Brandy for a bit, I prayed with her. She hugged me for far longer than was normal, but I didn't balk at it like I normally would have. The woman needed comforting.

"You saved my life," she whispered when she finally pulled back and wiped her cheeks. I started to protest, but she shook her head.

"No, I mean it." She smiled, but it was more of a grimace. "The doctor gave me Ativan to help calm me down so I could sleep, and I was planning to take... all of them," she admitted. My eyes widened and she nodded.

"Yeah. Today, as a matter of fact." She motioned to the sofa behind her. "I was just sitting there, trying to figure out what I wanted to say in my note when you knocked." Another smile lifted the corners of her mouth, this one more genuine.

"I think God sent you here to me."

Chapter 16

BRANDY'S STATEMENT had me reeling as I left her house and headed back to the bakery. I'd wanted to argue, to tell her I was just investigating a death because I was a nosy old woman with no faith in our police, but I certainly didn't want to take any wind out of her sails.

I grinned when I saw Jonny's car coming toward me and wondered if he'd figured out the ring's inscription yet. It was possible, since "Brandy" was a rather unusual name and the woman had been to the police station several times since J.T. had gone missing. I waved at the man, who surprisingly waved back, though with less enthusiasm.

"At least he used all his fingers," I mumbled. I wouldn't have been surprised if he'd given me the "Hawaiian good luck sign."

I signaled to make a turn on Oriole so I could avoid the downtown traffic, then had to slam my brakes on when a cat trotted across the street.

"Stupid creature," I grumbled. "Doesn't he know—" I paused when I looked a little closer and saw that it was an orange tabby with a white tip on its tail.

Like I'd told Maggie, a lot of felines fit the description of the missing cat in the newspaper, but as I watched the thing hop up on the curb and continue running down the sidewalk, I realized I recognized her. I rolled my window down.

"Bixby!" I yelled, eyes widening when the cat actually sped up to a full run.

A car honked behind me, so I made the turn, then slowly followed the cat. She had a destination in mind, that was for sure, because not even a barking dog slowed her steps.

For a moment, I lost sight of her, but then saw her tail behind a row of neatly trimmed row of hydrangeas. I kept one eye on that tail and another on the road before me. Thankfully, Oriole was a residential road with mostly retirees, so there weren't any children out playing to worry about running into the street.

We were almost to the cross section of Wren when the cat turned and ran up the front walk of a stunning colonial. The manicured lawn and pristine condition of the home spoke of wealth. I parked in front of the house across the street and watched as Bixby clawed at the front door and howled.

My mouth dropped when Eleanor Rogerson opened the door. She was the girlfriend of my former enemy, Mack Lawless, the man I'd erroneously blamed for my husband's death.

"Caramel!" she cried as she bent to scoop the cat up, hugging her to her chest. "Where have you been? Oh, my baby! I'm so glad you're home."

I got out of the car and crossed the street. Eleanor didn't notice me at first, since her teary face was buried in her cat's neck.

"Eleanor?"

She looked up at me and I nearly laughed when I saw that Bixby's... er, Caramel's loose hair had plastered itself to the woman's wet cheeks.

"Maddie? What are you doing here?" Eleanor's eyes widened. "Did you bring my Caramel to me?" she asked with a wide smile as she invited me in. I declined, explaining I needed to get to the bakery.

"That cat found her way home by herself." I explained how we'd come by the cat, how Maggie had suspicions it wasn't Allen's cat, et cetera. Eleanor shook her head.

"Caramel never leaves the yard. She'll go as far as the edge of the sidewalk, but never any farther. I have no idea how that Allen person could have taken her."

I pursed my lips. "My question isn't how, but why."

Leaving a very happy Eleanor after she said she wanted to call Mack to tell him the great news, I continued to the bakery, my head full of even more questions.

SATURDAYS WERE always busy at the bakery, though mostly in the mornings with people wanting donuts and the like. It was nearly noon by the time I got there, and the place was still crowded, despite the construction noise coming from next door. Todd's crew was making nice progress on our new pet café. He said it would be done in a week, which I didn't doubt, since they worked six days straight.

Jasmin gave me a tired-looking smile. "Hi Gramma," she called out as she refilled a coffee cup while simultaneously handing another customer his credit card and receipt.

James caught my eye then when he came out of the back room carrying a muffin tray. Judging by the oven mitts he wore, I assumed he'd just baked them. It was a good thing Maggie made up extra batches of dough before her days off, though it meant our huge refrigerator was constantly packed with trays waiting to be baked.

I laughed at the apron he was wearing. It was Maggie's favorite—hot pink, edged with frilly ruffles and "Is it hot in here or is it just me?" emblazoned in huge letters on the front.

"Did you lose a bet?"

The kid grinned at me as he slid the muffins onto the display tray and Jasmin giggled. I looked at her as I came around the corner, then headed to the sink to scrub my hands.

"He's a clown," she explained. "He'd do anything for a laugh." She gave the kid a fond look. He grinned back at her as he put the tray into the display case.

"Only because I love to hear you giggle."

My eyebrows rose as I caught Jasmin's eye. The girl blushed so hard, I was a bit worried that ring she had in her eyebrow was going to melt. I laughed as I went back to my scrubbing.

While I helped wait on customers, my mind was on the case... mostly the big question of why in the world would Allen have taken Eleanor's cat and then claimed to have raised her from a kitten? I figured he must have wanted to paint himself as some sort of animal rescue hero, but why he would have wanted to impress Maggie—a woman at least twenty years his senior—was anyone's guess.

Todd walked into the bakery covered in construction dust. He stood just inside the door and motioned for me.

"What's up?" I asked the handsome man. His hair was a funky shade of gray with all the dust in it. "Do you want coffee?"

He shook his head, releasing a small cloud as he did. "I don't want to come in," he said with a self-deprecating smile.

"Coffee to go?" He nodded and I started to turn, but he stopped me.

"We need to cover that wall," he said, pointing to the shared wall with the shop we'd rented next door. "We're ready to cut the pass-through window."

I grimaced; there were five tables along that wall, and all were occupied, as were all the other tables in the bakery. It made my heart happy to see so many contented customers enjoying their coffee or tea and pastries. Maggie and I had created not only a profitable business, but one that seemed to serve the community in a good way.

After asking Jasmin to get Todd a coffee to go, I made the announcement of what we needed to do. I apologized, but no one was upset. In fact, all the customers helped rearrange the tables, moving them closer together, then went back to their socializing, though I noticed they started talking to the other tables as well.

It was nearly closing time when Maggie walked in. I looked up from the sink where I'd been scrubbing pans when I heard the door chime. I smiled.

"How did rehearsal go?" Not that I cared. The idea of King Lear being made into an eighties musical still didn't sit well with me. I'd resigned myself to the fact that I was going to have to see it when it opened to support Maggie; I just hoped they didn't give her a singing part. The woman caterwauled like a cat in heat on a hot summer night.

She mumbled something I didn't catch, so I turned off the water and grabbed the drying towel. "What was that?" I asked as I turned to look at her, surprised to see she'd sat at the counter, rather than coming around.

It was then I noticed her expression and her pallor. "You look like you've seen a ghost," I told her as I stepped up to the counter in front of her.

Maggie startled at that and turned her wide eyes to me. She nodded. "I did," she whispered.

I sighed as I gave her a look. "Let me guess... King Lear?" Knowing Maggie and her penchant for hysteria, she'd probably seen the actor in costume and made the assumption the tragic king had come back from the dead... forgetting the fact that Lear had been a product of Shakespeare's imagination.

She shook her head and looked at the counter. "No." I frowned, wondering why she wasn't telling me what I wanted to know. Usually, Maggie blurted out all kinds of nonsense.

"Well, who was it?" I said with more exasperation than I should have.

She brought her eyes back to mine. "Allen."

Chapter 17

"ALLEN ROGERS?" I asked, just to make sure we were on the same page. Maggie nodded.

"And you're sure?" Another nod. I frowned. "How can you be so sure?" It wasn't like he was a life-long friend that she would know in an instant. She barely knew the guy.

Maggie swallowed hard and I took pity on her. I pulled a bottle of orange juice from the cooler and set it down before her. She just stared at it.

"When I saw him on Pelican, I yelled his name, and he looked right at me. Then he freaked out and took off."

My frown deepened. "Was he driving or walking?" I didn't know why I was asking the questions. I knew Maggie had to be losing her mind. What there was to lose, I wasn't sure.

"He was on a motorcycle," she whispered. "I didn't know ghosts could drive."

"It wasn't a ghost," I snapped, then sighed. "Let's start from the beginning. I assume you were coming from rehearsal?" She nodded.

I stared hard at her. "And was today rehearsing the part of the play where people die?" Knowing Maggie, she'd gotten overwhelmed by the acting, and conjured thoughts of ghosts.

I was surprised when she denied it. "No, today we just worked on the set and costumes. I was in charge of painting fairies."

"Fairies? In King Lear?" I waved my hand. "Never mind, I don't want to know." There was no telling what other liberties that Angelina woman was taking with poor Shakespeare's work. Like the music bit wasn't bad enough.

"Where exactly did you see Allen?"

Maggie frowned. "On Pelican."

I sighed again. "I know that, but where exactly?"

Understanding dawned. "Oh, at the light."

Apparently, the sun hadn't quite breached the horizon. I put my hand up and pinched my nose between my forefinger and thumb. "Which light?"

"Uh, Wren."

Well, that didn't help at all. That area wasn't in the touristy part of town, which is what I'd suspected—that Maggie had just seen a tourist that looked like Allen. Of course, it still could have been a tourist out cruising—

"He was on one of those motorcycles that jumps hills."

Maggie's weird comment brought me out of my thoughts, and I frowned again. "What in the heck does that—"

"You mean a motocross bike," James said from behind me. I glanced over my shoulder at the kid, eyebrow raised.

He grinned, not at all intimidated by me, darn it. "That's what Miss Maggie meant. A motorcycle that can jump hills is a motocross bike." He shrugged. "That's the kind I wanted when I ended up with that one," he added as he hooked a thumb over his shoulder toward the front window, where his motorbike sat in front of the bakery.

I considered that, remembering that he'd mentioned something about the bike he'd wanted had been stolen or something. I turned toward him. "Where was it that you said that bike had been stolen?" I asked. "The, uh, the motocross bike you wanted."

"Old man Charlie's," the kid said. I nodded. Robert had said Charlie Franchetti lived near the area Todd had built his cabins. My mouth dropped and I spun around to stare at Maggie. It was her turn to frown.

"What?"

"I know who killed Allen," I breathed, then grinned and clapped my hands together.

Maggie blinked a few times, then tilted her head to the side.

"Who?"

"Allen."

Her confused frown deepened. "Yes, Allen. Who killed him?"

"Allen."

She huffed out an exasperated breath, while I grinned. I'd always loved the *Who's On First* skit. But I held up my hand before she could ask again.

"Allen killed Allen," I clarified. "No, I don't mean suicide," I hurried to add when I realized what that sounded like. "I mean, he faked his death."

Maggie's mouth dropped open. "But... but who was that—"

"J.T. Oberlander," I said with a wince, when I realized poor Brandy was going to be even more devastated when she found out her husband had died.

"Who?"

I waved my hand. It didn't matter. All that did matter was that the police caught Allen before he took off, since Maggie had spotted him. I yanked my phone out of my pocket and called Robert.

"Hey, Sweetie Pie Cake—"

"Call Jonny and get some cops out to look for a guy driving a motocross bike," I interrupted. "It's Allen Rogers."

"What in the—"

"He faked his own death," I went on. "I'll explain later. Just tell Jonny that you figured it out, or else he'll never send anyone." It irked me that the kid refused to realize I was a better detective than he'd ever be, but in the moment, time was of the essence.

Maggie's eyes were still wide when I looked back at her. "Why would he fake his own death?"

I pursed my lips. "Well, if all Edwin said was true—and I have no reason to doubt it is—then Allen was in a heap of trouble with his publisher. It might've seemed like a better idea to just fake his death than it was to finish the book." I couldn't imagine that, but who knew what the man was thinking.

A whistle drew my attention. James was shaking his head. "That's some crazy stuff, like what you'd see on TV."

"Or in a book," I agreed with a nod, while my mind went back to that awful bit of writing I'd seen on Allen's laptop. Maybe it was a good thing he hadn't finished the book, what with how poorly it had been written.

He certainly wasn't a very good death faker, either. The "evidence" he'd planted around the cabin had been far too obvious. The man didn't seem to have a mysterious bone in his body, as far as I was concerned.

But he had fooled me—and everyone else—up to this point.

My phone rang, drawing me out of my thoughts. "Hello?"

"Jonathon actually listened to me, for a change," Robert said by way of greeting. "Kid even got the State Police involved."

I made an appreciative sound. "Just for a faked death, huh?"

"No," Robert said, drawing out the word. "If you're right and Allen faked his death, then we have a murder on our hands."

I nodded, then felt foolish, since he obviously couldn't see it. "It's J.T. Oberlander," I told him.

There was a long silence, so long that I checked my phone to make sure the connection was still solid. Then I heard a drawn-out sigh.

"Maddie, what else—"

"The ring," I interrupted. "The inscription, remember? Well, Maggie and I went to the Floydsville library and checked newspaper articles—"

"You know you can get a phone app for that," he interrupted. It was my turn to sigh dramatically.

"Anyway," I drawled, ignoring his suggestion, "there was an article about a woman—Brandy Oberlander—whose husband went missing the week that Allen supposedly died. I remembered the name 'Brandy' being on the ring. And her husband's name was Jerome... J.T."

Robert whistled, much like James had earlier. "Woman, you are turning into quite a detective."

I wanted to preen at the praise but forced myself to stay focused. "I bet if they check that blood on Allen's car, they'll find out it's Oberlander's," I went on. "I'm guessing Allen hit the guy with the car, put him in the trunk, then drove him back to the cabin where he... well, you know."

Robert hummed and I could tell he was thinking about what he'd just learned. "Richard did tell me the fingerprints on the trunk of the car matched Allen's."

"Why—"

"Before you ask, Allen Roberts had been arrested twelve years ago for check fraud," he explained. "That's why his fingerprints were on file."

"Did Dickie talk to Victor? He'd told me that the burned body had broken bones... like it had been in an accident."

Robert made a disgusted sound. "Why in the Sam hill would—"

"Victor seems to like me," I interrupted, already knowing what he was going to complain about. "He thinks I'm a better detective than Jonny." That wasn't exactly what the coroner had said, but I was sure it was true regardless.

"That may be, but he shouldn't be sharing info like that," he griped. "I'm going to have to have a talk... never mind," he sighed. "It's not my concern." I heard a sound that led me to believe Robert was rubbing his face, likely in frustration.

"You should just go back to the force," I snapped. "The Good Lord knows they need you." It wasn't the first time I'd said as much, though Robert kept insisting he was too old.

"Maybe just on a consulting basis," I rushed on. "And you can use me and my detective talents," I teased, but was surprised when Robert didn't laugh.

"It's a thought," he said, shocking the compression

173

stockings right off my varicosed legs. "I'll think about it."

I heard a voice in the background, but when I heard a police code, I realized it was his police radio. I couldn't make out exactly what they were saying, but Robert sucked in a sharp breath.

"Maddie, lock the door," he blurted. "Get in the back room. Now!"

"What?" I cried as I looked around the bakery. The afternoon crowd had mostly filtered out, but there was still a couple sitting at the corner table near the wall Todd's crew had covered with thick plastic, along with Nando and Alice, who'd become daily regulars thanks to Jasmin developing a soft spot for the old couple and insisting on giving them a ride to the bakery.

"I mean it, Maddie," Robert barked. "Whatever customers you have, tell them they have to leave immediately and then you and the girls get in the back room and lock the door. I'm on the way, and so is Officer Largo."

I wanted to roll my eyes at the last bit; Rick Largo was barely out of the academy, and I doubted he'd had to shave yet. But instead of arguing against a pimple-faced cop coming to my rescue for whatever purpose, I instead did as instructed.

"You need to leave!" I called out to the couple as I rushed around the counter. "And hurry. I don't know what's going on, but the police are on their way."

Jasmin ran around the counter to help Nando, who'd jumped up to help Alice while the other couple rushed out of the bakery. I locked the door behind them and turned to the elderly couple.

"Get in the back room," I said, then looked to Jasmin. "Make sure the back door is locked." We had a bad habit of forgetting to lock it since we were in and out so much, taking our garbage to the trash bins out back.

"Too late for that," a male voice said. We all turned to see Allen standing behind the bakery counter with a gun pointed at Maggie.

I gasped at the sight of my friend in mortal danger. It hadn't been that long since the Fishhook Killer had done the same. And it really ticked me off.

"What in the world do you think you're doing?" I snapped, hoping to draw his attention to me. "Have you completely lost your mind?"

Truthfully, he looked like he had. He was pale, dirty and shaking, with several weeks' worth of scraggly beard that made him look like he'd been ambushed by a herd of Daddy Longlegs who'd taken up residence on his chin.

"Don't," Allen said, almost a plead. He shook his head. "Just don't. I'm… I'm desperate."

I harrumphed. "No kidding. Only a crazed and desperate lunatic would point a gun at sweet Maggie there. You should've gone after me instead."

When he swung the gun my way, I stiffened. It was one thing to be brave when he'd been threatening my best friend, but quite another when I was on the receiving end of it. But it was necessary to keep Maggie safe. *If I can.* I knew how quickly things could go badly and how it was entirely possible Allen was going to kill everyone in the bakery.

His next words confirmed that.

"I can't have witnesses," he said, his voice shaking nearly as much as the hand that held the gun. I wondered if he was on some kind of drug.

"Maggie saw me," he said, his wide eyes swinging back to my friend. Her back was to me, but from her posture, I knew she was as stressed as I was. "I can't have witnesses," he repeated as he started to turn the gun back toward her.

"So, what?" I barked, hoping to draw his attention again. "You're going to kill everyone here?" I swept my hand out, indicating Nando and Alice, who'd sat back down, with wide eyes trained on our attacker. Allen looked their way, seeming to be surprised to see them.

"You're going to kill three old ladies and an old man just

because you want to get away with faking your own death?"

His eyes widened again, as if he were surprised I'd figured it out. I rolled my eyes. "It's kind of obvious, since you're standing here."

Allen swallowed and rubbed his free hand over his face. Maggie reached out and picked up her juice bottle, which caught his eye. The gun was turned on her again. Surprisingly, she shrugged.

"Thirsty," she said nonchalantly as she tried to twist the cap off. She struggled with it for a bit, then sighed dramatically and set it back down.

"I'm assuming you were planning on framing Edwin for your 'murder'," I said with air quotes, thankful when his attention turned to me again, though the gun remained trained on Maggie. "But I knew it wasn't him. You left too many clues. Way too obvious," I smirked, like I was the expert on framing someone.

"But you missed J.T.'s wedding ring," I went on. Allen looked a bit confused, and I wondered if he'd even known the name of the man he'd killed. "The man you burned to death," I clarified.

Allen shook his head almost violently. "I would never have done that," he said. "He was already dead then."

"How did you get Edwin's lighter?" I asked. My out-of-the-blue question caught him off-guard and he answered automatically.

"He'd left it on the table at a book signing," he said, answering the question of where he'd gotten a signed copy of Edwin's book. "Evans was my hero," he continued in a near-whisper, as if he'd forgotten we were there. "I wanted a memento."

"One would wonder if that was the beginning of your criminal career, but we know it started even earlier." My tone held enough chastisement to make the man squirm. "Let's not forget about the check fraud."

Allen coughed, then swallowed. "I was desperate," he repeated in a near whine. Maggie drew his attention when she grabbed the bottle of juice, once again struggling with the lid for a moment before plunking it down with a huff. He glanced at her with a slight frown.

"Why did you steal that cat?" I demanded. Once again, I think I shocked him with the out of the blue question.

"I needed someone to check on me," he said as he looked at Maggie again. "I knew if I didn't come back after the week we agreed on, Maggie would come looking. I needed someone to find the body."

"And how did you know the whole cabin wouldn't burn down? You could have been guilty of burning half the forest down, for crying out loud. What a moron!"

That drew his attention back to me, just as I'd wanted. He pointed the gun at me again with a scowl. "Todd told me the cabin was built with fire-resistant materials. That's how I came up with the idea. It was a brilliant plan," he protested, then jerked his head Maggie's way. "If she hadn't seen me earlier, I would have gotten away with it and Evans would be locked up!"

"And why were you trying to frame Edwin?" I demanded as I caught movement out of the corner of my eye. Jasmin was trying to sneak Alice and Nando toward the back room, and I wanted to give them a distraction.

I took a step closer and pointed a finger at him. "You're just jealous of him, that's what I think," I taunted. "You couldn't stand seeing all the success Edwin has. It ate at you and made you do crazy things, like buy a bunch of your own books."

Allen looked like I'd slapped him. "How—" he shook his head, then scowled at me. His hand was a lot steadier as he raised the gun and pointed it right at my head.

"Just shut up," he snapped. "I don't know how you know all this, but—"

"Because you planned this as poorly as you plotted your books," I sneered. "Any idiot would have figured it out." I didn't mention the fact that I hadn't figured it out until Maggie had

177

sworn she'd seen Allen, but I was sure I would have figured it out eventually. Hopefully.

"Shut up!" he screamed. I guess I had pushed him just a little too far. So, I decided to push him even further.

I held up a hand. "One—find out Edwin is coming here for a retreat and get the harebrained idea to frame him for murder. Two—kill some innocent man so you have a body—"

"I didn't kill him," Allen protested, running that hand over his face again. "That part was an accident. He was out walking, and I accidentally hit him."

"I doubt it was an accident," I bit out. "You were looking for a victim. You needed a body. And even if that wasn't the case, hit and run is just as bad." I shook my head in disgust, then continued my countdown.

"Three—steal some poor cat and claim her as your own just to have someone find 'you'. Four—decide all that isn't bad enough and add cold-blooded murder to your list," I said, pointing at the gun, then dropping my hand to plant my fists on my hips.

"You're pathetic, Allen Rogers. You're a horrible writer, so bad you had to try to steal another man's success by imitating his name, and you're an even worse person. Shame on you."

His face fell at my chastisement and for a moment, I thought he was going to drop the gun and give himself up. But after a second, his face hardened.

"That's enough," he growled, and I knew that was the moment he'd decided he was at the end of his rope. And it was the end of the line for Maggie and me.

"Dagnabbit!" Maggie yelled, drawing both our attention. She had the bottle again, held against her chest as she tried to get the cap off. "This sunny beach just won't come off!" She made quite a show of trying to screw the cap off.

Allen cursed as he roughly grabbed the bottle out of her hands, then slammed the gun on the counter so he could open it. Like a flash of lightning, the gun was in Maggie's hands. She jumped off the stool and backed away, all while pointing the weapon at him.

"Hands up, you... you... poophead!"

I couldn't help but snort out a laugh at that pathetic excuse for a bad name. Allen put his hands up, still holding the juice.

A second later, a bang in the back drew all our attention. We watched as Rick came tripping in through the back room of the bakery, gun swinging wildly as he tried to figure out what was going on.

"Hold on there, Barney Fife," I called out. Of course, that comment just caused a confused look on the young officer's face. I had to assume he had never seen *The Andy Griffith Show.*

"Don't go shooting anyone just yet." I pointed at Allen. "This is the one you want," I said as I reached out and pushed Maggie's hands down, pointing the gun at the floor. I was surprised she wasn't even shaking.

"Good job, honey," I murmured to her. My compliment startled her, and she looked at me, then gave me a slight smile.

"I didn't like him pointing the gun at you," she whispered.

"I know," I told her. "I felt the same way about it pointing at you."

Robert and Jonny arrived at the same time, though Jonny tried the front door first. I glanced at him, giving him a little wave. I could have easily unlocked it for him, and we both knew it. The look he gave me before he ran down the sidewalk was priceless.

My man quickly assessed the situation, then hurried around the counter. He took the gun from Maggie, then gave her a quick hug, before pulling me into his arms for a better one.

"I was never so scared in my life," he murmured in my ear, "as I was when I heard that Rogers had doubled back and was headed toward this end of town. I just knew he was coming here." He reached down and pulled my hand up. My eyes widened when I saw my phone was still connected to our call from earlier.

"I heard everything. Just about had a coronary." He gave me a little squeeze. "Woman, you have *got* to quit antagonizing the murderers!"

I laughed as I squeezed him before stepping away from our hug. "Well, it worked, didn't it?" I nodded toward Maggie. "But the Academy Award winning actress over here had the idiot fooled and managed to get the gun from him."

Maggie looked at me in confusion. "How did I fool him?"

I scrunched my mouth to the side. "With the juice… pretending you couldn't open it."

"That wasn't an act," she said with a head shake. "I really couldn't open it."

I huffed. "Well, at least you snatched the gun up."

She grinned. "I did do that."

Robert laughed as he patted Maggie's shoulder. "I'm thankful no one got hurt."

Jonny came in through the back room then and gave me a glare before assessing the situation like his grandfather had already done. *What a boob.*

I left the boys to it as I headed around the counter to check on Jasmin, Nando and Alice. The three of them were chatting and giggling, like a near-murder hadn't almost taken place. Jasmin promised to take them home, then I wrote out a sign for the front door saying we were closed for the rest of the day. After saying our goodbyes to the others, Maggie and I left in her car.

"Well, that's another case solved," I told her when she stopped at a traffic light.

She smiled at me. "I wonder how much money we'll get this time."

I pinched my lips together. "None," I said. "The last one had a reward, but the only reward for this case is the satisfaction of solving it before Jonny could." Not that he really could, but still.

Her smile turned to a pout. "Poop. I was hoping to donate to Angelina's theatrical projects."

I half-turned in my seat. "Is she hitting you up for money?" That made my blood boil, finding out that my suspicions about the woman were true.

"No," Maggie shook her head. "She just asked us for donations."

I had to work hard to keep my eyes from spinning like a slot machine wheel. "That's what 'hitting you up' for money means, ding dong!"

"Oh," she breathed.

"Yeah, oh." I sighed then as I stared out the window. "But if there had been a reward, I would have used my part to help Elle. Somehow." There wasn't really any help for my daughter, I knew. But if there was anything at all—

"We're going to take care of her," Maggie assured me once again, interrupting my thoughts. "Don't worry about that." She glanced at me, though the light had already changed. The car behind us honked.

I smiled, though Maggie didn't see it since she was thankfully paying attention to the road and traffic.

"I appreciate that," I told her. "More than you'll ever know."

Maggie turned her head to grin at me. "I think maybe we should concentrate on the cases that actually pay a reward," she said before returning her attention to the road ahead. "That way, we'll have plenty of money to take care of Elle." She cleared her throat and looked my way once again.

"She deserves it," Maggie added, making me smile.

"That she does," I agreed. "But you don't need to worry about that," I went on. "It's my duty to—"

"I want to," Maggie interrupted as she signaled to turn. "I never had kids of my own," she whispered. "I can't imagine how you feel."

I swallowed hard against the lump that crawled up my

throat. Instead of answering, I just nodded, though Maggie couldn't see it since she was thankfully paying attention to the road for once.

"Well, I appreciate it," I managed to repeat, though barely. I was a bit emotional after our ordeal. And of course, just thinking about Elle hurt my heart.

Maggie hummed as she drove down our street. I stared out the window at the houses, realizing I only knew a few of our neighbors, despite having lived there for over five years. It was ridiculous, really, considering we lived in such a small town. I need to quit being so reclusive. I decided to talk to Maggie about possibly baking up some goodies to use as an introduction.

"So... what's next?"

I startled at the question and glanced at Maggie. "What do you mean?"

She shrugged, then signaled to turn into our drive. "I mean, what should we do next? What case should we work on?"

I laughed. "Well, I guess we need to wait for another body to show itself." Of course, that made both of us cringe. "I mean, not that I want someone else to die," I added quickly.

Maggie shut the car off and we climbed out. My car was still missing, so I figured Jasmin had taken Nando and Alice to the store, which she did often. My granddaughter acted like a better Christian than I did, yet I doubted she laid claim to the faith. *Something else I need to do... talk to Jazz about Jesus.*

I slammed the door a little too hard and Maggie scowled at me. "Sorry. Used to my heavy doors." Wally was at the front window, wiggling happily as he watched us approaching.

"Can't wait until Todd finishes the pet cafe," I laughed when I saw Samuel Adams jump up on the windowsill, then proceed to walk back and forth in front of the dog. Maggie laughed too.

"That cat sure loves Wally. Can dogs and cats be boyfriends and girlfriends?"

I gave her a look as she opened the front door. "Well, they can be friends, obviously," I said as both Wally and Sam ran over to us for scratches and pets.

"Oh, who's my good boy?" I baby-talked while Wally acted like he was going to lose his mind, as he always did whenever I came home. It could be five minutes or five hours, and he always acted with the same craziness.

I straightened when Wally stepped over Sam to get some love from Maggie. "But they can't be, uh, animal lovers." That bit of info should have been obvious, but it was Maggie, after all.

"Well, what should we do for the rest of the day?" I asked as we both headed into the kitchen by unspoken agreement. For some reason, I was famished. *Must be from the adrenaline rush before.*

"There's a Monsters of the Deep marathon," she suggested as she filled the tea kettle.

I didn't have to respond as I pulled the fixings out of the fridge for turkey sandwiches. She knew how I felt about those ridiculous movies she loved so much.

"Or maybe a few episodes of *Magnum, P.I.*?" She grinned, knowing she'd said the right thing.

"Yep, that's the ticket." Tom Selleck could grace my television screen any day of the week.

Maggie's phone rang then, and from her end of the conversation, I could tell she was talking to Edwin, filling him in on all that had happened. While I was a bit surprised the man had called her—and that he even had her number—I can't say I was unhappy about it. It was about time Maggie had a man who was interested in her, instead of the other way around.

And the fact he was my favorite author didn't hurt either.

Once we were settled on the sofa eating our lunch and watching Magnum chasing after an extortionist, I sighed happily. Another case solved, another feather in our own private detective hat, and another murderer—or at least bad guy—off the streets, as they say.

Life was pretty darned good.

Pfeeet

I slapped my hand over my nose. "Oh, for crying out loud!" I cried when my eyes started watering. Maggie winced and glanced my way, as Wally whined and got up to leave the room, heading down the hall to Elle's room.

"Sorry," she shrugged. "Had crabcakes today."

I waved my free hand around, then took a tentative sniff. Thankfully, the stench had dissipated. "You really need to expand your diet," I told her. "You can't eat at Kirby's every single day."

"I don't," she protested. "Just a few—"

"You know what I mean," I snapped, then sighed. "Sorry, let's just enjoy the show."

Several minutes went by and I returned to my pre-stench happy zone. Everything just seemed to be falling into place in my life, I realized. With the exception of Elle's horrific disease and the fateful outcome of that, everything was good. And even in Elle's case, I was grateful she was with us where we could do all we could to make her comfortable.

Robert and I were happy. We got along better than I ever had with anyone else. And, yes, that included Frank. In fact, I had a secret wish that Robert and I had been together instead of Frank and I.

I was especially happy that Robert had started attending church with us. He even liked it, and liked Pastor Winchester. I was still holding that man at arm's length, but it was a mutual distancing. We'd silently agreed to disagree.

The bakery was doing fantastic, to the point we really needed to hire more people. And with the addition of the pet café, not only would we increase traffic even more, we'd get to have our furbabies close by.

Yes, life was certainly good.

Pfeeet

I sighed. Most of it was good, anyway.

I hope you enjoyed *Lying Tongues & Frosted Buns!* If you did, would you be so kind as to leave me a review? Reviews are like writer hugs and let us know that maybe we should continue doing what we're doing!

If you'd like updates on what I'm up to, please join my newsletter at http://eepurl.com/hoasyb. I offer freebies, writing samples and soon... more recipes! Come join us; we'd love to have you!

Recipes

Here are a few recipes mentioned in the book. I hope you enjoy them! (I can't have sugar, so I'll enjoy some of them vicariously through you)

Maddie's Meatloaf

Loaf:
1 lb ground beef
1 lb breakfast sausage
1/4 C chopped onion
1/4 C chopped bell pepper (or green chile)
1 ½ teaspoons salt
1 ½ teaspoons freshly ground black pepper
3 slices bread, dry (or toasted) and crumbled; or, alternately,
    ½ package of saltine crackers, crushed
1 egg, lightly beaten
3 tablespoons sour cream
2 tablespoons Worcestershire sauce
1/2 C tomato sauce

Topping:
1/4 C ketchup
2 T yellow mustard
1 T Worcestershire sauce
4 T brown sugar

(alternately, you may substitute a good BBQ sauce for topping. We use Sweet Baby Rays sugar free!)

Preheat oven to 350. Mix all ingredients well. Press into a bread pan (or 8x8 square pan). Bake 50 minutes.

Meanwhile, combine ingredients for topping. After 50 minutes of bake time, remove loaf from oven and increase oven temperature to 400. Pour topping on loaf, spreading evenly. Return to reheated oven and bake another 15 minutes. Let cool 20 minutes, then slice and serve.

Macon Bacon Donuts

4 tablespoons butter, softened

1/4 C vegetable oil

1/2 C sugar

1/3 C brown sugar, packed

2 large eggs

1-1/2 teaspoons baking powder

1/4 teaspoon baking soda

3/4 teaspoon salt

1 teaspoon vanilla extract

2-2/3 C all purpose flour

1 C milk

Topping

6 slices bacon, cooked, cooled, and crumbled into small pieces

1/2 C diced peaches

4 tablespoons maple syrup

Glaze

1 cup confectioners' sugar

1/4 C maple syrup (or enough to make a spreadable frosting)

Preheat oven to 350°F. Grease two standard doughnut pans (or bake in shifts if you just have one pan).

In mixing bowl beat together the butter, vegetable oil, and sugars till smooth. Add eggs and beat to combine. Stir in baking powder, baking soda, salt and vanilla.

Stir the flour into the butter mixture alternately with the milk. Make sure all ingredients are mixed well.

Sprinkle bacon and peaches evenly in donut pan wells. Drizzle maple syrup over that, about 1 teaspoon per well. Spoon batter evenly in the pan(s), filling the wells up to the rim.

Bake for 15 minutes until donuts are raised and a toothpick inserted in the middle comes out clean. Remove from oven and loosen edges of donuts with a knife or spatula before turning out onto parchment or waxed paper.

Glaze: Stir confectioners' sugar and enough maple syrup to make a spreadable glaze. Spread over donuts.

Serve warm, or at room temperature. Wrap any leftovers loosely in plastic, and store for 1 day at room temperature; refrigerate or freeze for longer storage.

Blueberry Lemonade Bars

Crust:

2 C all-purpose flour

1 C butter, softened

1/2 C white sugar

Filling:

1 ½ cups white sugar

¼ cup all-purpose flour

4 eggs

2 lemons, juiced

Topping:

1 8 oz package cream cheese, softened

1/2 C butter, softened

1 teaspoon vanilla extract

3 C confectioners' sugar

1 tablespoon milk

1/2 to 1 C blueberries, rinsed and patted dry

Preheat the oven to 350 degrees. For crust, mix 1-1/2 C flour, butter, ½ C sugar in a mixing bowl until combined. Press into ungreased 9x13 inch pan. Bake in the preheated oven until firm and golden, about 15 minutes.

Meanwhile, for filling, whisk remaining 1-1/2 C sugar and

1/4 C flour in a medium bowl. Add in eggs and lemon juice. Beat until smooth, then pour filling over baked crust. Bake another 20 minutes. (Crust will firm up as it sits.)

While crust cools, make topping: Mix all ingredients except for blueberries until creamy and smooth. Carefully fold in blueberries. When bars are cool, frost with topping and cut into squares.

OTHER BOOKS FROM VJ DUNN

Haughty Eyes & Alibis, Book 1 of the Church Lady Mysteries

When Wally Wonka—my best fur friend—found a body in the woods near our church, it became clear Jonathan Donovan, our local police detective, is utterly incompetent. Maggie—my best human friend—and I decide to take matters in hand and do a little investigating of our own. After all, how hard could crime solving be?

Beginning the End Book 1 of The End Series

My name is Nikki. Just a country gal with no real mad skills. But after the global economic collapse, my husband Reg and I found ourselves leading a ragtag group of survivors, those who managed to escape the cities...and the Neos. The Neo Geo Task Force is the new government. The new world order. They were supposed to be the law of the land, the peacekeepers. They were anything but.

Surviving the End Book 2 of The End Series

This time, our present, was the end of the age. Or, at least the slippery downward slope heading toward the end. My name is Nikki and with my husband Reg we tried our best to protect our growing group of survivors. Everything that happened had been foretold in ancient texts, some written long before Christ walked the earth. But even knowing the prophesy didn't completely prepare us for just how difficult those times would be.

Embracing the End Book 3 of The End Series

While the rest of the world was celebrating the establishment of the "new world order," we were struggling just to eat. We fought to live, to exist. We never could have imagined just how bad things would get. But betrayal was our worst enemy. The Lord never left us, though. His promises kept us going, gave us direction. He led us and guided our steps, even when those steps took us right up to the Neos' doorstep. And then we were no longer fighting. We were storming the gates of Hell.

Conquering the End Book 4 of The End Series

The hunt continues. But now the entire world is after us. We are Followers of The Way—believers of the Christ. Our enemy, the Neos, have morphed into something even worse than the demon-possessed Satan minions they were. Now they rule the world and their quest is to annihilate anyone who stands in their way. Which means us. We know that Christ wins in the end; we just have to survive until then. We just hope the last day comes quickly, because the earth is going to Hell.

The Releasing Book 1 in the Reign of the Lion Series

The End Series continues with Allie and the Remnants in the Millennial Period. It's been nearly one thousand years since the Tribulation, and it's supposed to be a time of peace. But Allie is up to her eyeballs trying to deal with backtalking Remnants, arrogant angels, a joking Abba and an annoying growing affection for her right-hand man. And of course, there is the small fact that Lucifer is going to be unleashed on the world soon...

The Tempting Book 2 in the Reign of the Lion Series

While Satan oozes his fake charm to gather all those who might turn to the dark side, Allie has her hands full — an unruly team of Remnants, a man who keeps her teeth grinding and hormones raging, a pet bobcat who couldn't keep her nose out of Allie's business, angel warriors who insist on doing things their own way...and, oh yeah, that pesky angel rebellion to deal with.

The Gathering Book 3 in the Reign of the Lion Series

Never in a million years would Allie have ever guessed that she'd be part of Lucifer's tempting of those born in the Millennium. But after being captured by the gorgeous Prince of All Things Slimy, she was not only a part of it... she was the biggest tool in the evil dude's arsenal. By keeping her bound under the paralysis power Allie had come to despise, Lucifer assumed she was completely under his control. Powerless. Helpless. That was his biggest mistake yet.

The Consuming Book 4 in the Reign of the Lion Series

Allie isn't thrilled with her new assignment. It means putting herself in danger of being captured by Lucifer once again. But this time, she won't be a captive--she'll be an example. She'll do her best to follow Abba's wishes, but she knows it's not going to be easy. Witnessing to Lucifer's army is not exactly going to be a church picnic. To top it off, she has the upcoming war with said army on her mind. At best, they'll be able to win the army to Abba's side, to salvation. At worst? Allie's head will become Lucifer's new war helmet.

Falling Book 1 in the Saints of Salvation Series

Coming to grips with his own mortality was difficult enough, but coupled with a complete economic crash that sends the world spiraling into an abyss of doubt and fear, Nathan Diamond has no idea what to do next. His best hope is to get his wife out of the city... and fast. As Nathan struggles with his body's deterioration while on the run. he can't help but question the existence of the God his wife so desperately seeks. Tammy prays often--and loudly--whenever they're faced with a crisis. And when her prayers are miraculously answered one after another, Nathan finds his beliefs being reshaped. But is it too late for a dying sinner to find salvation?

Hiding Book 2 in the Saints of Salvation Series

The world as we knew it has ended. No surprise there; the Scriptures warned us about this for thousands of years. And yet... we were shocked. Unprepared. Devastated. Now we're on the run. It's not easy. We have to hide from the others, those with evil on their minds. Sometimes we have to fight against them. Do what it takes to make it through. Our only hope is to find other people like us. Those who know what's going to happen. Believers. Together, we might stand a chance. We just have to survive until then.

Warring Book 3 in the Saints of Salvation Series

They thought they just had to hide. To survive. To live. They had no idea they were going to have to fight. When the Lord sends His messengers to prepare you to battle the enemy, you have a tendency to listen. But when those messengers tell you to storm Hell's gates... things get a little scary. But there are innocents at risk. Those who refuse to give in to the enemy, who refuse to take the mark of the beast. They shouldn't have to suffer just for being obedient to God Himself. And now, the little band of misfit Christians valiantly fighting against impossible odds is their only hope of escape. Thankfully, God works in the impossible.

Waiting Book 4 in the Saints of Salvation Series

The group of followers were told by God's very own angels that they were to go to Israel. But when the enemy throws everything he can at them to stop them, doubt creeps in. What if they misunderstood? Should they just hide and wait out the Tribulation? Was it possible that the angels were working for the enemy, trying to distract them or mislead them? When GOD remains silent to their pleas and questions, the little band of survivors begin to turn on themselves, to turn on their leaders. Fear threatens to override common sense. Will they be able to keep them from tearing each other apart... especially when they have Satan himself to battle?

Soul Pirate, Book 1 in the Restless Soul Series

When a pastor finds that his church and family have turned against him when things didn't turn out like he'd preached they would, *The Pastor* wanders from place to place, trying to find a purpose for his life. But can he survive long enough to discover his place in a world turned upside down?

Tight Fittin' Jeans, Book 1 in the Story In A Song Series

Connor is a man without hope. His world is crashing down around him and while he *has* been praying for a miracle, it seems that his prayers are hitting the ceiling. Evelyn is lonely, married to a man who considers her little more than a means to the end. She feels duty-bound to complete the task she's been given. But her heart isn't in the job—instead, she longs for adventure. For just one night, she wants to pretend she's simply a "good ol' boy's girl." When Connor prayed for a miracle, is it possible that Evelyn is the answer to that prayer?

Mama's Heart Book 1 in The Tapestry Series

Misty is shocked to learn she's pregnant, and out of wedlock too. But all things work out, until a fateful day when her entire world is turned upside down. Misty becomes bitter, angry, and questions everything she ever knew about God. But a surprise visit from a stranger helps her put life into perspective and to see God's handiwork in weaving the tapestry of her life.

Unanswered Prayers Book 2 in The Tapestry Series

Steve Tyler is the typical mid-western kid... a little nerdy, very smart, with a great future. Through a series of life-changing events and "unanswered" prayers, Steve turns his back on God and turns to drugs for his comfort. Homeless, friendless and hopeless, where every day is a struggle just to survive, Steve finds himself in such a deep valley that the only way up is by taking God's hand. A meeting with a stranger might just be the hand up he needs.

Here, Hold My Beer, Confessions of the Common Sense Challenged Male

Stories that will break your funny bone and keep you in stitches... and you won't have to go to the ER! Humor satire about the dumb things that guys will sometimes do. You know, those decisions that usually start with a trip to the liquor store and end up with a trip to the hospital. If you like to hear those "chill around the fire pit, guzzling six packs and spitting tobacco at the flames" kind of stories, this book is for you!

Made in the USA
Middletown, DE
06 December 2022

17275406R00116